Drowning in the Streets

Melanie Rose Hirshberg

PublishAmerica
Baltimore

ISBN: 1-4241-4533-3
PUBLISHED BY PUBLISHAMERICA, LLLP
www.publishamerica.com
Baltimore

Printed in the United States of America

Thank you to My Friends. My Life.
You know who you are.

For Mom and Dad
None of this would have been possible without you.
I love you.

1

The lights of tall buildings below her were like bright stars against the darkening skies outside her window. Her heart pounded inside her chest and she felt like a child discovering the wonders of her little world again. This was the first time she had ever been on an airplane, or on the coast (or anywhere outside of Wisconsin for that matter). She was glad that she was experiencing it with the one she loved. She looked at her husband.

He had been watching her. He smiled and it made her tingle all over. It was still hard for her to believe that they were married, Mr. and Mrs. John Olsen. *Mrs. Kelly Olsen.*

"It's not fair. Don't they care that we just got married?" asked Kelly solemnly.

"Not so much. A week is all they could give me. I warned you when we met. But it's not like I won't be back soon...Maybe we could start making a family then?" he finished with a devious smile.

"By then we'll be an old married couple," she pouted. She thought of the three-day "honeymoon" they had at the local hotel. "Besides, I don't know if I'm ready yet."

He sighed and agreed, even though he wanted to point out they were almost thirty. He wanted to point out that one of the things that had driven them together was their love for children. He wanted to point out the fact that he had always dreamed of having four children – two boys and two girls—because he didn't want his children missing out on what he had with his lack of siblings. He didn't though. What he did point out was that the buildings were growing closer—they were descending.

The rest of the time the couple sat quietly, squeezing hand in squeezing hand, as their excitement climbed up their spines. They were more nervous than they had ever been before, but it was a good nervous. It was a nervousness of ancient adventurers who wondered what new discoveries were next to come around the corner.

At the airport, Dana Smith, their landlord, was waiting for them. She was to take them to their new apartment, which she had sold them via Internet. She was the one who had sent them photos and made them fall in love with the apartment. Kelly had always imagined her as a magnificent woman – tall, beautiful, and gallant. In reality, her hair was fluffy and gray and stuck out in most directions. She was rather short and plump as well. She reminded Kelly of a squirrel right before winter, when they were fattened up for the cold.

As they took a cab to the house, Kelly took in everything around her. She knew that cities were home to many people; she had been to Madison and Milwaukee many times and read books and articles on the subject, but nothing had quite prepared her for this. She had grown up in rural Wisconsin, and she thought for sure there would not be as much poverty as she had seen in some of her neighboring towns when she went for community service projects. The times that she had been in cities, she had only seen nice homes and nice people. But maybe she just hadn't been looking in the right spot.

Once, when she was much younger, her oldest brother had told her about a time when he and his friends had gotten lost in the city. He told her of drug dealers and prostitutes, but she had thought he was just trying to scare her. Even when she became a nurse at a local hospital, she never saw cases of overdoses or gunshot victims.

On some streets there were people of all ages putting away signs that read 'I'm a Veteran' or 'Help the Homeless' or rushing into buildings before night completely fell. On other streets tough-looking kids clad in baggy clothes pushed each other or stood in dangerous-looking groups or hid in the shadows, waiting…There were small children in worn out clothing playing under the glow of a streetlamp with no shoes on their feet and no apparent guardian. Kelly noticed a little girl of about five who seemed skinny enough to hide behind a string bean.

"Is it like this everywhere?" asked John, glancing worriedly at Kelly.

"No. Just wait until we get to where we're going. It's *much* nicer there."

Within five minutes, they were in a new neighborhood with brick buildings two to four stories high. Clothes hung out to dry from upper-story windows. Well-to-do adults lounged on stoops and watched little ones as they played tag up and down the sidewalk in t-shirts and jeans and light-up sneakers. The cab pulled into a spot and they got out. The couple looked up at the building in front of them. It was brick like the others, three stories, with white trimming around the windows and with an elegant Victorian style front door.

"As I've told you before, you have the bottom two floors and I have the top. Most of your belongings arrived last night and is already in the apartment. The movers said the rest should be here by tomorrow afternoon." Then, in one swift motion, she picked up a suitcase and unlocked the door, leading John and Kelly inside. Before entering, Kelly looked back the way they had come. A few blocks down a large group of people stood huddled under a streetlamp, a cloud of smoke glowing eerily above them. She wondered just where her "nice" neighborhood ended.

Inside was warm and cozy unlike the chilling night air (despite the ninety degrees it had been earlier that day). They were in a foyer that had a door leading to the left, and presumably the downstairs apartment, a door leading outside to the right, and a long, dark, looming staircase leading up. Dana unlocked the door to the left and disappeared into blackness that reminded Kelly of a cave she had once explored as a teenager. The light turned on. After her eyes had adjusted to the change in light, Kelly gasped quietly. She felt herself being lifted and John was carrying her through the doorway into a spacious living room.

"It's so much more beautiful in real life. This is so…so perfectly amazing," she breathed as her feet touched to the ground. John grasped Kelly's hand and squeezed it gently. She could feel the joy in his grip. Her body tingled all over; this was their first, and hopefully long-lasting, home.

"I suppose you want the grand tour. This is the living room or den or family room or whatever you might want to call it. Through that door is a bathroom. If you follow me this way," Dana called as she led them through a doorway, "This is the kitchen." Kelly's breath was stolen away when she entered the kitchen. It was large, only slightly smaller than the living room, with a refrigerator and stove already in it, and in the corner a black spiral staircase led up to the second floor. The second floor was much larger than the first because it went over the foyer. "This is where the bedrooms are. The master bedroom is at the end of the hall and the two rooms on this wall are also smaller bedrooms or whatever you'd like to change them into. That door in between the smaller rooms is a linen closet and this a second bathroom right here. In the basement are a washer and dryer, but I would appreciate it if you bought your own detergent. The empty half of the basement is your storage space. The door's under the stairs. Here are your keys, and just give a yell if you need me. Oh, and please keep the outside doors locked at all times. You always have to be careful."

"Of course," answered John in a low voice. Kelly led Dana back to the door through a maze of boxes, with John in tow. "Before you go, I noticed a door across the hall leading outside? Is there an alleyway there?"

"Oh, yes, I'm sorry, that leads to the alley next to the building. That's where you can put your garbage. The garbage men come around on Wednesday mornings and recycling comes Mondays. Well, good luck. I'll see you in a few weeks, John and Kelly I'll see you soon." Then she retreated up the dark stairwell and the newlyweds were alone.

"What do you want to do?" asked Kelly.

"Why don't we set up the bed?" whispered John as he traced his finger down Kelly's spine.

When Kelly awoke the next morning, John had already gone downstairs. He sat on the window seat, facing out the large, alcove window in the living room. She put her hands on his shoulders comfortingly. His whole body sighed under the weight and it seemed that he was an old man.

"You'll be back soon. Don't worry," she soothed.

"That's not what's wrong!" he answered defensively, though it was easy to see through him. "I just realized I missed the big game last night while we were on the plane."

"Oh, sure," she let out sarcastically. Then she added, "I know how you are about your basketball."

"You mean baseball, right?"

"Oh yeah, I'm sorry. You're right. Baseball is in summer and basketball is in spring, right? I never was any good with sports."

An hour later John said good-bye and left Kelly alone with her thoughts. She wondered what he would do if he ever found out that she actually knew more about sports than he ever could. By the time she was eight she had learned every rule to every major sport and could list *all* of the players on *all* Wisconsin teams *and* their positions.

She tried unpacking boxes for a long time, but she kept getting distracted by thoughts of her wedding and her husband and it just wasn't fair…Just as she was settling herself on the cushioned window seat to think, there came a knock at the door.

"Dana! Hi! How are you?" exclaimed Kelly in surprise when she discovered her neighbor behind the door. She was glad to take her mind off John.

"I'm fine. I'm going to the market and I thought you might like to come and stock up on supplies."

"That would be great," agreed Kelly with a small nod. She went to get her purse and two minutes later they were exiting the house. Down the street the same group of people was standing under the same streetlight. In this light, she could tell they were kids. And, today she saw that there was another group there too, across the street from the former, and it seemed to her that they were yelling to, or at, each other.

2

Down the street, nine-year old Kid Jax, a.k.a. Lane, was sitting on the stoop of an old, run-down apartment complex, watching the two gangs, The Jokers and The Panthers, yell at each other. He enjoyed watching them fight. He found it almost comical how they always challenged each other, but no one ever dared to cross the street alone, especially not in broad daylight.

In fact, in his four years there, he had never actually witnessed anyone cross the territory line. Once, two years earlier, a member from the Panthers across the street had crossed the line, and something bad had happened. Something he had been too young to understand. It put three of The Jokers in jail, including the gang's leader, Ghost. It had been almost a miracle that The Panthers hadn't retaliated, because with three in jail and no real leader, The Jokers would have been crushed quickly and easily.

Kid Jax, fondly called Jax by most of The Jokers' members, shifted his small body to get a clearer view of his friends. Will, his brother, had told him to stay close to them. ("If there's any trouble, Hawk and The Jokers will help," he had said. Kid Jax didn't quite know what he had meant by *Trouble*, but he was hoping he didn't run into any.) He vaguely wondered what Will had done to make *Trouble* come. Then his stomach grumbled, and his thoughts turned to food.

He had figured out a while earlier that Will had gone for food. Jax hoped he would bring something good, but he knew that there was only a slim chance of it actually happening. Even though he tried the best that he could to provide for them, living on the streets was hard enough and finding enough food for two was even harder, especially when the elder was sixteen. He was too old to be young and cute and too young to be trusted- people thought of him as bad news, just like The Jokers or any other teenage male from that part of town, whether justified or not. If they were really starving, Jax could beg on a street corner in the nicer sections of the city, no matter how much Will hated bringing him into it. *He* was still young and cute and people were more generous to him than his brother. Very rarely did they go into a soup kitchen, and then Will would pretend to be eighteen so neither would be taken away from the other.

Jax's stomach was growling louder and louder at the thought of food, and it was so distracting to him, that it took him a long time to become aware of the stranger blocking out the light of the sun. As he looked up, the man shifted so that he was outlined with a bright light that blinded Jax. Putting his hand up to stop the sun, Jax finally focused on the strange man's face – a dark, straight face, with equally dark eyes and a slit turned into a frown. Without looking directly at Jax, the man started speaking.

"You the one they call Kid Jax?" he asked. His voice was very deep and it reminded Jax of the kind of thunder that came only moments before the sky opened up and all Hell broke loose.

"Maybe," Jax answered in a small, but threatening voice. "Who wants ta know?"

"Tell Snap that Dean wants the money. And if you don't…" the man let himself trail off. Everything is more threatening if you let it trail off. Will was always using the technique when he wanted him to be good.

As his throat went dry with fear, Jax wondered if this was what Will had meant by *Trouble*.

"Who's Snap?" the boy asked in false confusion. In reality, he knew all too well that Snap was his brother. Jax *also* knew that it was usually better to "bend the truth," as Hawk loved to say, with these kinds of people. Especially when they were over twice your age and about three times your size. Any extra time you could create, the better.

"You know who he is!" the man growled deep in his throat. He took a threatening step toward him.

"Ooh, you mean *that* Snap! Yeah, sorry, it must've slipped my mind. Sorry 'bout that mix-up and all, you see my mind's not so great. No schooling and all," Jax returned coolly, inching back on the stair. The man was obviously mad now, and Jax gulped as the sun beat down on him making him feel like bacon sizzling on a pan. The man took another step towards him, and the kid jumped up, putting the length of the stoop between them. The gang was to his back now, and he only hoped that someone would look over and realize something was going on. "Yo, mister, I didn't mean disrespect or nuttin'. I just didn't know. You don't have to get mad."

"I'm not mad. I'm just s'posed to make sure the importance of this message gets to your brain…and your brother."

"You really don't have to do that, mista. I get the importantness of it right now," Jax returned as cool as possible when someone's scared to death. The man took another step towards him, and Jax sprinted for all his life in the other direction – to the safety of The Jokers.

He could hear the man's heavy footsteps behind him; one large step for two of his. He was catching up. The gang had not noticed what was going on, but Jax could see them standing calmly underneath the same streetlamp they always gravitated towards. The Panthers must have left. Jax tried to call out Hawk's name, but nothing came out.

Suddenly Jax got the sensation of leaving his body, and then that he was falling to his death. The last thing he saw before he hit the ground was one of the gang members, he was falling too fast to see which one, pointing in his direction.

Nothing cushioned his fall except his hands, which he had outstretched to lower the blow to the face, and a few weeds growing between the cracks of the pavement. He hit his head. Hard. He rolled onto his back to try to ward off anything the man might try to hit him with. Everything went silent to him and the man looked almost magical, towering over him like a giant. The man kicked him in the side and grinned. Then he ran. What seemed like hundreds of legs surrounded and passed the dazed Jax. They followed the man, but a few bringing up the rear came to his side.

"You all right, Kid Jax?" asked one of them. His voice sounded so far away and Jax couldn't process who it belonged to. He couldn't focus on their faces either. One of them helped him sit up and he winced from the pain in his side, but it wasn't as bad as it could have been. The man must not have kicked him as hard as he could. The gangsters around him talked to one another, saying things like 'he doesn't look so good,' and other palpable statements. He wished they would shut up while he got himself together. Besides, they were just giving him a headache.

Most of the gang came back shortly. Jax still sat in a state of confusion. Then he heard another voice from the gang. He wished he could figure out who was talking.

"Dawg, is Jax okay?" asked the young man with the heavy city accent.

"Dunno, Hawk. He's not talkin'. Someone get 'im a drink," Dawg answered with his own, untraceable, accent. And then everything came rushing back to Jax. Of course it was Mad Dawg. Jax had always thought it was ironic (though in simpler terms) that Mad Dawg, his personal favorite of the gang, had that name when he was one of the nicest people the boy knew (though his acquaintances were limited). Hawk on the other hand was much scarier, if not very protective of him and his brother.

"I…I'm fine," Jax stammered as his mind cleared. He shook his head hard – trying to clear it. Little bits of dust flew from it.

"You sure, Kid?" asked the same one who had talked to him first, Sam. He was still new to the gang and hadn't earned a nickname yet.

"Hey!" he snapped seriously, making Sam jump. "That's Mr. Kid Jax to you!" Jax smiled. "'Sides, I coulda taken him if I wanted. I was testin' all your skills." His fear was now hiding inside so none of the guys would know he was really shaking. He wished his brother would get back soon. Until then, he couldn't be calm.

"He's fine," laughed Mad Dawg and helped him up. If Hawk knew otherwise, he kept it to himself. Instead, he watched Mad Dawg and their young friend taunt Sam. A small twitch in his lips gave the hint of a pensive smile, but no one but him could be sure.

Meanwhile, Kelly and Dana had just finished all of their shopping. They had gone to the supermarket and then to the quaintest farmer's market. It was held in a small park where red and white roses and colorful gardens made Kelly forget for a short time about the dreariness of the city. Farmers from outside the city had set up rows and rows of stalls full of fruits and veggies.

Now they were window-shopping on their way home down a street full of fascinating buildings and people. The buildings looked old, with gargoyles peering disapprovingly down at them like guards of an ancient castle. The girls chatted cheerfully and for the first time Kelly thought that she and Dana could possibly become friends. They had many things in common – although they did not share the same decorating style. Kelly was more contemporary while Dana was…not.

"Oh, look at that! That would look so wonderful in my kitchen, don't you think?" Dana asked enthusiastically. Kelly looked through the glass at the bright yellow, green, and blue spotted ceramic chicken.

"Um…yeah. I'm sure it would look…lovely in it. It sure is…uh…bright."

"Perhaps I'll buy it another day. First I will have to figure out where to put it. I have these kinds of things all over my apartment. Maybe I will put it next to the pink and purple duck, or the fuchsia cow," Dana mumbled to herself.

Kelly rolled her eyes discretely and shifted all her grocery bags to her left hand. *And how lovely it must be,* she thought to herself and giggled.

The sidewalk was crowded and it was hard for them to stay next to each other, but they managed somehow. Both were completely caught up in their conversation, unaware of the teenager slowly coming up on their right. Not until it was too late, anyway. In a flash of movement the boy was there, then disappearing into the crowd again. Kelly gasped and then yelled as she realized he had taken her purse. But by then, it was too late. The boy was gone.

After they had given their statements to the police, Kelly and Dana walked home, despite the officer's offer to drive them. Kelly was calmed already, and she just wanted to get away from the questions and noise. Dana kept apologizing for bringing Kelly there and she promised that the city would get better. It was only bad luck, she said. But Kelly wasn't overly worried anymore; after she calmed herself earlier she had realized there wasn't much worth taking. If her purse didn't show up in a couple of hours she would cancel the credit cards, and she had only had $60 in it.

Then, they got to the house, and they both gasped. Kelly's purse was sitting on the front stoop, seemingly untouched by anyone. Kelly put down her groceries and ran to the purse. She was so intent on getting some answers she did not notice the shuffle of movement coming from the alleyway.

"How much is gone?" asked Dana nervously.

"Twenty dollars…only twenty dollars. I had sixty in here. That's so weird…" Her sentences had all but trailed off.

"Yes, it is." But Kelly wasn't listening anymore. A piece of paper at the bottom of the purse had caught her eye. She lifted it out and examined it.

"What is that?" Dana asked curiously.

"I don't know. A note. It says 'Sorry for taking this. I had to. I got a brother. Sorry. Snap," she answered so quietly that Dana had missed everything except 'I got a brother' and 'Snap.' Kelly was stunned. He had returned it. On the other side of the paper, the faded remains of a Lost Cat sign could be seen.

The two went inside and separated into their respective apartments, despite Dana's insistence that she should stay with Kelly. *You're in shock*, she had said. And maybe she was because she found much joy in being allowed to put away her groceries in any spot she chose. After, she decided to take a nap, but she couldn't get her mind off the boy. As she lay on the couch, she kept picturing his face ad then the note and on and on. Only a split second had gone by in which she had seen his face, but it was sticking to her like glue.

He had maybe been eighteen, probably younger. His dark brown hair had come halfway down his ears. It had been dirty and stringy and had fallen over his dark eyes. He had been around 5'7", give or take a couple of inches. But the most important thing she remembered was his clothes. They had been dirty and worn. They were worse than any she had witnessed the night before.

On the note, the last sentence had only said 'snap.' What did that mean? Was it a name or a trademark or some kind of threatening gesture?

All of this thinking had worn her out and eventually she fell asleep.

Will had come and gone again. Jax had seen him coming up with a bag in his hands. There had been a turkey sandwich the size of his head with a pickle, chips, and a soda in it. He had asked Will what he had gotten. Will went uncharacteristically silent and told him to not worry about it. Then he told him that he had gotten some water for later that he was going to put in their "mansion." After tousling his little brother's hair, he had left. Jax hadn't seen his brother since. Even so, the short time Will had been there helped Jax get his courage back. The way that Will spoke to him always made him seem brave and invincible.

Jax had wandered around the block and back. The Jokers were no longer under their streetlamp; they had ventured off to do whatever it was that they did. It was pretty late in the day as far as he could tell and he was again getting hungry. The worst days were when he got to eat because that just left more to want. Now he probably wouldn't eat again for a while, they would leave their canned food stash for when they *really* needed it, unless Hawk or Mad Dawg got something extra to share. That was rare, though; they had their own families to support; besides Will would never tell them when they were starving unless Jax himself was getting sick.

No one else was on the street. Usually, there were a lot of people outside their apartments, sitting in the sun or playing in the streets, but not today. Today it was too hot for the old men and women, and much too sunny for the little children. Besides, today trouble was out.

He was deep in thought about the old life, what he could remember anyway, when he became aware of footsteps behind him. At first he shook them off as just some people walking the streets. When the steps continued, he couldn't help but turn around and look. There were four people – men—

following him, but he only recognized one. And he sure didn't like who it was.

"Remember me?" the man growled with the same vicious grin on his face as the last time Jax had seen him. "Guess what? Your brother hasn't gotten back."

"Uh…no speak English?" Jax bolted as fast as he could down the street. He hadn't gotten a good look at the others, but he was sure that they were just as strong and just as big as the other one. Jax screamed all the names he could think of: Hawk, Mad Dawg, Sam, and Will, even Snap. He called the names of the other gang members, too, even Deuce who had once threatened his life for stealing his seat.

The men taunted the boy's cries, they wanted him to give up, but he would not. This time the young boy had gotten a large head start, and he was a little stronger and stronger willed from the food—his thoughts of bacon earlier had made him yearn for it and now he vowed he would eat it again, just to keep himself going. He ran as fast as he could for blocks, barely noticing a very old woman closing her shutters as if to ward off a storm. He could barely breathe. Stronger, yes, but nowhere near what he used to be like. Right before he thought he was going to collapse, he turned into an alleyway. This would at least give him a few seconds to hide before the men came to find him.

3

Kelly was awakened by noises outside. She ran to the window to see what was the matter and was shocked to find a small boy being chased by large, dangerous-looking men. She gasped and crossed herself. She vaguely wondered what the boy could have ever done to make these men so mad, but all she really cared about was his well-being. No matter what had happened, he could not possibly deserve such impossible odds.

The little boy was red in the face. He was wearing old jeans that were too big for him and that had holes in their knees-which were actually at his shins, and a green sleeveless shirt that for some reason made her think for a moment of Chachi from Happy Days.

In contrast to the tiny boy, the men were giants. But they were a good distance behind him. If he made the right moves he could lose them. He passed under the window. She wanted very much to give some sign to him, to show him that he had somewhere to go. Then, in a miraculous act of coincidence, or fate, he turned into her alley. She glanced back at the men-they were still half a block down, and slowing, because they must have known it was a dead-end. She bolted across the hall and opened the side door.

"Kid! Where are you?" she hissed loudly. "Come in quick! They're almost here!"

Jax didn't know if she could be trusted, but she looked a lot safer than the men, who even then he could hear nearing the alley. He jumped out from behind a garbage can and used his last ounce of energy to sprint into the building. The woman quickly locked the door behind them. They stood listening to the men as they came into the alley. Then, silently, Kelly motioned for Jax to follow her.

Jax didn't move. He knew not to follow just *anyone*. But she was young and very pretty. She smiled. He was in her living room before he knew it.

"You'll have to mind the mess, sorry. My husband and I just moved in yesterday. All of our stuff isn't even here yet," she explained cheerfully, but awkwardly. She obviously didn't want to make him nervous. She was trying to be trustworthy. He wouldn't let himself give in too easily, though, no matter how much he wanted to. It wasn't twice a day Jax could be hurt. "Are you hungry?"

He was sold.

Jax nodded and she led him, trailing a cautious foot and a half behind. He sat on the counter while Kelly went about and made sandwiches for him. He graciously took a sandwich and then two others. He finished it off with three cups of milk and a glass of lemonade. Kelly took this time to take in his appearance.

He was very small, but she guessed that he was older than he looked. His eyes were cheerful, but they had edges as cold as the icy blue they were. His hair was dark brown and down to his ears. He reminded her of someone. His skin was like tanned leather from too much exposure to the sun. She tried to imagine him as a pale little boy with delicate skin. She watched as his eyes deepened into a scowl and he concentrated on eating. Was he memorizing the taste?

Finally, he finished eating and she thought it was safe to talk.

"I guess we haven't officially met. My name is Kelly Olsen. What's your name?" Kelly paused to give him a chance to answer. He eyed her suspiciously. "All right. That's okay; you don't have to tell me. Let's see…what can I tell you about me? You know I have a husband. He's in the Marines and I'm a nurse, but I haven't found a job here yet. My parents are back in Wisconsin. That's where I grew up. Where did you grow up?"

Jax decided that he could tell her. She wouldn't be able to figure out anything useful with that information. It's not like she could track down his parents or anything. "Jersey. Been here four years."

"How old are you then? Ten?" she guessed. He was apparently small for his age, and she figured he wouldn't have considered it 'growing up' if he was much less than 5 when he left. He shook his head no. "Nine?" He didn't nod, but his eyes brightened a great deal. "That's a good age. I remember being nine. I'm twenty-nine now. It seems like a very long time ago."

"My name's Kid Jax."

"Kid Jax? That's an interesting name."

"It's Lane. Kid Jax is sooo much cooler though. Or Kid or Jax for short if you want. Usually Jax, though. That's what the guys call me, anyways."

"The guys?" Kelly asked. Jax nodded. He wasn't sure if he should tell her about them, she might not like them like she liked him. They were a lot older and bigger and scarier. After a few moments of silence she went on. "So, where do you live?"

"In the city," he answered vaguely.

"Where? Close-by?"

"We usually live near here." So he was homeless.

"We? You mean you and the guys?"

"No way!" he laughed. The food seemed to have finally kicked in with his energy. "We! Me and my brother. Will. The guys live with their families. No way would they live with us. Sometimes they sleep with us. Well, not with us. Just with us. You know, when they get into a fight with their parents or somethin'."

"How old is your brother?"

"Sixteen. He turns seventeen soon though. What day is it today?"

"The fourteenth of July."

"Oh."

"Oh?"

"Just wonderin'. What does that clock say?"

"It says 6:27 PM. Don't you know how to tell time?"

"Not so good on those kinds of clocks. He's tried, but I don't get it. I have to go now. My brother likes me back before night."

"Are you going to be okay? What if those guys are still there? Or if they come back?"

"They won't be. Besides, someone will be under the light."

"Okay," she answered with a nervous smile. She knew what light this tiny child had been referring to; it was the same that boys—much larger than him—always seemed to be under. No, not boys – what he called "the guys", and she called 'the gang.' She wondered if the gang had caused the trouble to come. But even if that were true, she knew from the way he had spoken about them that they would protect him. She didn't think they would cause trouble for him on purpose.

"Could I take some? I don't want to steal them or nothing, I just don't think he got enough. Just enough for me. And water. Without water you die you know."

"Yeah, I know, but who didn't get enough what?" She had been distracted by her thoughts.

"Food. My brother Snap didn't get enough food," he answered absentmindedly. Kelly froze. Snap? Had she heard him right? "Are you all right? You're pale. You look like he does when he's sick."

"Yeah. Fix whatever you want. Anytime you want, you can come over and just get a little something to eat. Or anything. To talk or to take a shower. Even if you need a place to sleep. Your brother can come if he wants, too. Snap you said?"

"Yeah. That's what the guys call him anyway. I usually just call him Will. Maybe I'll come back. I like it here," he said as he piled layers of ham and cheese onto two end slices of bread.

He hugged Lane long and hard. Lane handed him sandwiches. He decided not to ask about them until after he had eaten – no use tarnishing a good thing. No, a great thing. He didn't think he would ever know the feeling of winning the lottery, but as he bit into the ham and cheese, he did. He hadn't eaten in almost a week, with the exception of a Twinkie that he had mooched off of Hawk a few days earlier. And besides that, he hadn't eaten ham in much, much longer. He couldn't remember the last time he had eaten it. He could remember having it every day for lunch at school, though. Maybe that was the last time…

Of course Lane and Hawk didn't know – nor would they ever. They thought he ate every time Lane did. But he never took enough money for that. Like today.

When he had taken that woman's purse, he had only taken enough money for one meal and water…and an extra ten dollars for the pay off. As soon as he had gotten what he needed, he had taken it right back to the address in her address book. He had even stayed and watched it to make sure no one else took it. He couldn't just let anyone take her purse. He had too much of a conscience to do that. *Not much of a street rat, am I?*

"Lane, where did you get all this food? And how come you're not eating?" Will eventually asked, leaning against the wall. He was full for the first time in ages.

"After those guys chased me I hid in an alley and the woman there let me in her apartment to hide. She gave me food and told me if we ever want to go back we can. We're allowed! We can use her bathroom if we want. It smelled really nice."

"Huh? That's great," he returned not caring. He had no wish to use some stranger's bathroom. The public one in the deli was fine for him if he needed it. But she at least seemed legitimate, but something was making him uncomfortable—"What guys chased you? You didn't get yourself into any trouble did you?"

"I don't know. The guy from earlier today was there."

"What guy from earlier? You didn't tell me about any guy earlier," he said sternly. He felt like he was going to throw up.

"The guy with David or Dane or whatever."

"You mean Dean?" he asked. He fought to keep his food down.

"Yeah. That's it."

"What did he say?! God, why didn't anyone tell me?!"

"He said he wanted his money back. What did he mean by that?"

"Nothing. Just forget about it. I'll deal with it tomorrow." He closed his eyes and pushed hard against the cold wall. Stay calm. Stay calm. Change the subject before he asks more questions. "So this lady, tell me about her."

And so he did. He talked about her for over an hour until he passed out mid-sentence. Will carried him onto their "new bed," a mattress Drac from the Jokers had given them when his mom threw it out the week before. It was a huge relief from the old worn out mattress they had used for so long. He lay down next to his brother. It was chilly out, and he wished that fat bum hadn't stolen the quilt that Ghost had given them so long ago. During those first days.

4

The next day Snap, stripped of all of Will's sentiment, walked straight up to Dean's lair, and the 300-pound man guarding the entrance. He felt the money in his pockets and hoped it was enough to keep the man off his back. It was only about half of what he "owed," but it was absurd to think he'd be able to come up with that kind of money in the time allotted. The huge man stepped aside and he entered cautiously into the old abandoned warehouse. It was dim inside, but a light shone on a desk. How cliché. Behind the desk sat a skinny man in his thirties. He wasn't scary in person, not even remotely, but he owned goons that were. Dean motioned for Will to sit down. He did.

"So, *Snap*, you have the money?" asked Dean in a calm, mock-Mafia voice.

"Yeah. Here," Snap answered coolly while fishing in his pockets. His hands were shaky and sweaty.

"Where's the rest of it?" Dean demanded after he had counted it.

"What do you mean the rest of it? That's it!" He knew instantly that he had responded too quickly and too defensively. He bit down hard on his tongue.

"You're over three hundred dollars short," he said with the same calm voice.

"Bull! That's all I had to get. I gave you a lot more than I took! You hurt *my* brother, now you claim I owe *you* more?" He clamped down again on his tongue. *Why can't I keep my mouth shut?*

"Are you saying I'm a liar?"

"Yeah, I am! Maybe five, ten dollars short, but not three hundred! I did not take five hundred dollars! What I gave you is how much you get!" A goon that had been standing behind him silently now stepped forward and slapped him in the back of the head. *Great, now I'm gonna get killed.*

"Now listen here," growled Dean, losing his suaveness. He leaned over his desk threateningly. "You get me the rest of the money by Saturday. I don't get off much hurting children, but there are always exceptions."

"Saturday! How do you expect me to do get that kind of money?" Snap yelled, allowing Will's desperation to seep through. Sweat was pouring down his back and all he could think about was Lane.

"I hear you're friends with The Jokers. Maybe they can help you, I've heard of some pretty nice jobs they've pulled. And if they like Kid Jax enough to help him against one of my guys, they must like you, too." Will's heart had stopped at the direct reference to his brother. He would get the money somehow.

He left numbly, with Dean's last words echoing in his brain; "Remember, no one misses a street rat."

But next Saturday came and he only had a hundred dollars. He had taken ten dollars here, twenty dollars there. No notes this time apologizing, just purses appearing and disappearing. No one else had the money, either, not Hawk or any of The Jokers. They had been planning a job for it, but Will refused. He wasn't going to have their troubles weighted on his shoulders, too. (Not that it would matter much once he was dead.) However, he did stay close to them all day and made sure that Lane was within their grasps at all times.

On the outside, Will put on his Snap bravado. He was loud and sarcastic, just like any other day, and he acted like he was invincible, but Hawk could tell it was an act. He knew that inside he was shaking and scared, and he knew that nothing would make him feel better. If only there was something he could do…

That night it was decided that Jax would stay in Mad Dawg's flat while Will stayed with Hawk. They could talk about their options then without fear of Jax overhearing. But first he had to get a mysterious something from 'The Mansion.'

"You want me to come?" Hawk had asked. "Strength in numbers and all that shit."

"Nah, it's all good. I'll be back in a minute."

"You sure?"

"Yeah I'm sure! Whad'ya think? I know how to take care of myself!" He was trying to convince himself.

25

"I didn't say that. Chill. Just stay alert, a'ight? And here, take this," said Hawk. He reached into his jacket and pulled out a small handgun.

"No, man. I got my knife, that's all I need." To prove his point, he took the knife from his pocket, flicked it open, closed it, and put it back, all in the blink of an eye.

"All right. Just be careful." Hawk watched as his companion headed down the street. After two blocks he turned onto another street and Hawk knew 'The Mansion' as they called it was only a few feet away. He stayed on the front stoop of his building, keeping an ear out for any signs of trouble. His hand was at the ready, just in case.

After what seemed like hours and still no sign of Snap, Hawk started to get worried. He decided to wait five more minutes, and then he would go. With his eyes and ears still alert, his mind started to wander. He remembered when his brother had found the brothers in the first days. By now, they were like his brothers, too. He never had enough money to help them, not like Snap would let him during normal circumstances, but whenever he could spare money he would try to help. His mother had never let the "street filth" over if she was around, even when Ghost had lived there, but tonight she was out with a boyfriend. He thought Snap would be safe there.

Five minutes was up.

Gun in hand, Hawk made his way down the street to where he knew the boys were living. The street was dark except for a lone streetlamp. Something underneath it caught his eye. A dark, thick liquid. He cautiously went closer. It had a red tint. He cursed loudly, causing pigeons to stir from dark shadows.

"Snap! Where are you? Snap!" he screamed, looking up and down the alley frantically. *Not like this...no way in Hell like this.* "Come on Snap! Will!" He ran through a gaping hole in the side of the boys' building, where he knew others would be squatting. He found many people inside, all of whose faces were hidden by shadow, but still gave truthful answers to his question. They saw nothing.

Hawk knew the blood was his friend's. There was no other option – he wouldn't have just left without telling anybody, and Dean wouldn't have taken him without bloodshed. No one else would be stupid enough to jump him on Joker territory. But there was nothing he could do now. The blood stopped under the light. There was no trail to follow.

Soon Hawk had the whole gang out looking for Snap. Mad Dawg and Hawk took Jax to search at Dean's lair after he fought tooth and nail not to be left with Drac's sisters. The Lair was pitch quiet, which made Hawk even more nervous. He knew that there was usually at least one guard outside the door and lots of activity going on, especially at night.

"Kid Jax, stay out here. Behind those boxes," ordered Hawk, referring to a mound of boxes behind them. Jax was on the verge of crying. He wished he had stayed at Drac's. He missed his brother already and he didn't want him to be hurt. For less than a millisecond he wondered what would happen if Will had died, but he pushed it away, not being able to fathom it.

The boys came out again, shaking their heads at Jax's question before it was even asked. He had not been there.

All night they searched to no prevail. Hawk led, Mad Dawg followed a few steps behind, Jax holding on to the leg of his baggy pants. He didn't care if he seemed like a baby tonight. He didn't care if they thought he was brave or not. He just wanted his brother back.

Then, just as the sun started to come up over the skyscrapers of downtown, they spotted something amongst garbage cans in a back alley. They were over a mile from the warehouse. Once again Jax was told to stay behind. Hawk and Mad Dawg cautiously made their way towards it, knowing fully well that it was a body (though whose they did not know). Hawk started running, and once coming upon it, cursed loud enough to make a dog bark nearby. A pit filled Jax's stomach and tears burned at the back of his eyes.

"Is...is it...?" he stuttered loudly enough for them to hear. Mad Dawg moved swiftly next to Hawk and they both kneeled down. They were talking to it so quietly he couldn't hear them. In fact, he couldn't hear anything. His world had gone silent.

He watched them for a long time, not sure what to do. Whoever or whatever it was, was not moving. Then, so suddenly Jax jumped back, the body stirred and a long, painful groan pierced the odd silence. He ran to them unthinking, and then, upon catching sight of it, stopped dead in his tracks.

It was Will—or something that resembled him, anyway.

5

Kelly wasn't expecting to see Kid Jax again. It had already been a week, and besides that, if she were a street kid, she probably wouldn't return to the same place twice. She had been nice, but in his eyes, what would have stopped her from calling child services? But still she worried. What if the thugs had come back? What if something else happened to him? What would they do in the winter?

She had told John a little about Jax and his brother when he had called her later that day. She had told him about the boy coming for sandwiches, though she did not tell him how he had come to be at their house. She left out the part about the men, and the purse incident, and their ties with the gang. She left out, too, the street name Snap, which sent shivers down her spine every time she thought of it. How did he get that name?

And even though he voiced his concern for her well-being and her feelings with great passion, she could not let them escape her thoughts. He didn't think the little one would ever come back. He thought he had conned her for food. She knew better. She had seen the fear, and then the warmth in his eyes. She tried to hold on to the hope of seeing him again.

Kelly was sound asleep when a strange noise entered her dreams; she opened her eyes to the soft yellow of an early sun across her pillow. The noise was coming from downstairs. There was a buzzing, and voices – frantic voices. *What's happened now?* It wasn't until she reached the kitchen that she realized the buzzing was her doorbell, which until this point had gone unused. She pressed the button to talk to whoever was at her door at 7:00 in the morning.

"Yes?" she asked groggily.

"Kelly! Kelly please let me in! It's real important! It's me, Jax!" came the voice from the other side. There were others behind his, how many she couldn't tell. His was very little compared to the last time she had talked to it. This time it seemed very young and scared, instead of the tough voice he had previously used to make him appear older and tougher. The others seemed older, but just as frantic as Jax.

"All right. Hold on. Calm down," she said in a faux relaxed voice. He sounded so scared. And who were the boys in the background? Were they friends or enemies? What was she getting herself into?

She opened the door and unconsciously crossed herself. Before her stood Kid Jax, tears in his eyes, and three teenagers behind him. Two of them, she instantly recognized by their clothes, were Streetlamp Gang members, and they held up the third – a very severely injured, barely conscious…he looked very familiar. Now she knew why they had sounded so frantic. In fact, she was getting frantic now, too.

"What happened? Come in; come in. Oh my goodness."

Kelly led the boys into her living room, where even more boxes and furniture had now been stuffed. She grabbed an old blanket from a nearby box and threw it over the sofa. "Put him down here! Jax are you all okay?"

"Yeah, just him. Put him on the couch. Quick come on," pleaded Jax, whose voice was quickly breaking. When the young men traded equally unhappy looks, Jax got exasperated. "Trust me, she's cool. She's a nurse. She can help!"

"Jax, what happened? How long has he been like this?" she asked while the others gave in and placed him on the blanket. All three boys were silent. "Come on, this is important. I need to know…otherwise I can't help him."

Jax stayed quiet, but the taller of the boys started speaking. "Well, see ma'am, he got beat up pretty good. We don't know by who or by what really. He was staying with him [he pointed to Hawk], but had to get something and he didn't come back. That was before one last night. We were searching all night. We found him a bit ago and we had to run here from 34th Street. We don't know how long he's been out there. More than a couple of hours I think, probably since before three. When we first found him he was out, then he woke up for a little. He's been going back and forth, ma'am. We couldn't understand what he was saying." All the while Mad Dawg had been speaking, Kelly was looking over the boy.

She studied his face. It was badly bruised and cut, but she knew this face. It was the same one that she had seen that day on the sidewalk. This was Snap.

This was Snap, but his injuries were too extensive.

"I have to get him to a hospital," she told Jax. But it wasn't Jax who responded. It was the young man who had not spoken yet; the one who, now that she looked at him, while small, was much more threatening than the big one. He had a fierce look and shadows for eyes.

"No! I told you she'd do this Kid! We can't take him to a hospital! Are you kidding me? Or are you just stupid? He's homeless for Christ's sake! What do you think they'd do? I'll tell you one thing, we'd sure as hell never see him again!" Hawk yelled fervently. Kelly jumped. He was shaking violently. She wondered vaguely if he was going to kill her now, but Jax turned on him angrily.

"Hawk! Shut up!" he yelled, overpowering all of them. Then, more calmly, "Kelly, we can't take him to a hospital! Don't you see? We'd be split up. It would be like…be like you and your husband never seeing each other again." He was shaking, but at least now the scary one wasn't. Now he was just watching Snap with a deep scowl. Jax continued in a pleading tone, "Can't you help him? You're a nurse…can't you help him?"

Mad Dawg turned to Jax and placed a hand on his shoulder reassuringly. Snap moved and groaned, which broke Hawk's spell, and he looked at Kelly, his eyes momentarily softened. None of them breathed until she answered.

"I can try. That's all I can do."

"Thank you," answered Jax quietly. He seemed very small again.

"I can't promise anything – if it's more than I can handle, I'll *have* to bring him to a hospital, otherwise there won't be a Snap for you to be apart from. Now Jax, get a towel from the bathroom, and the first aid kit and a washcloth from under the sink," she ordered, snapping into nurse mode. "One of you— get a glass filled with water, the thing of ice, and paper towels from the kitchen!"

Jax and Mad Dawg ran off, leaving Hawk and a nervous Kelly alone, but were back soon with the needed things. Kelly sent all of the boys into the kitchen to get something to eat and drink, and Hawk surprised her by complying. Once they were gone, she started examining in depth.

I'm in over my head, she thought as she pulled on her rubber gloves and tried to decide where to start. Next to the drunk driving accident, this was the worst case she had ever seen, and she had never been completely alone. He was barely recognizable under the injuries, and she hoped that what she could see was the extent of it and there was nothing internal.

There were tiny cuts around both eyes, from what she presumed was shards of glass shattering, and his whole face was black and blue and swollen. There were cuts in his mouth, too, along his gums and he had bitten his tongue badly. There was a cut below his chin, which was already scabbing over; but if it had been over mere centimeters, he might have already been dead. But all of that could wait.

His shirt was beyond any sort of repair, torn into scraps and missing large portions, but because of its natural burgundy color, the blood soaking it had gone unseen. She had to cut it off of him with medical scissors. What she found made her want to throw up. His stomach looked like a sadist's idea of a checkerboard. There were two parallel gashes going from the top of his chest down beside his navel, and three more going from rib to rib perpendicularly. They didn't seem to be deep enough to cause any problems to organs, but they were still bleeding. She got the towel and put as much pressure on his stomach with it as possible while still examining with the other hand. They would cause him a lot of pain when—if—he woke up. She prayed that there wasn't any internal bleeding underneath.

She turned him cautiously onto his side. His shoulder blades were bruised and scratched, as was his lower back, but it didn't seem too important. Turning him back, she took in the sight of his jeans—or what was left of them. They were completely shredded from the knees down. From what she could see, his legs, too, were badly bruised and there was a deep gash on his left calf.

She moved the towel to his leg and pushed down hard. He groaned in his sleep. *Good, he's responding.* She taped it down tightly and moved back to his stomach. She took the washcloth and wet it and cleaned out the cuts, then disinfected them and put large sheets of gauze tightly down on them.

She was looking over his arms (a hand shaped bruise around his wrist, some scrapes on the backs, and maybe a broken finger), when he started shivering. He had a high fever. She threw a quilt on top of him, leaving only enough space for her to clean out the leg wound and put tight bandages on it. She then washed off his face with the paper towel and put disinfectants along the cuts. They didn't even need bandages.

A crash came from the kitchen. Panicking that maybe one of them *had* been hurt and was now splayed out dead, she ran to the kitchen, still holding the paper towels. What she found was the teens sitting at the table looking sheepishly at Kid Jax, who had apparently knocked his glass of lemonade of the table and into a million pieces on the floor. He looked at her guiltily, but she really didn't mind. She was just glad she didn't have to fix anyone else.

31

She tossed him the paper towels and told him to be *very* careful cleaning up the glass.

She went back to her patient and sat on the edge of the couch. The cut on his leg had already bled through the gauze so she added more and held it down for pressure. With her other hand she checked his stomach wounds. They had all but stopped, which meant they weren't deep and that they shouldn't cause too much extra trouble, besides a lot of discomfort.

"He okay?" The voice came so suddenly that Kelly slipped off the couch. They both chuckled in spite of the tension.

"I sure hope so. I don't think he was out there for as long as your friend thought, though. He would have been a lot worse if he had." He nodded in semi-agreement.

"By the way, I'm Hawk," he said as he extended his hand to help her off the ground. She paused before taking it. "'Bout before, it's my job to make sure he's safe, that's all."

"I understand," she said semi-truthfully. "So, you're Hawk. Who's your friend?" asked Kelly, thinking of the way he had kept calling her "ma'am." She sat back on the sofa, checking the bandages again. Nothing needed to be changed. He wasn't shivering anymore.

"Mad Dawg. The name fools ya though," he said, warming a little. "He's one of the nicest sons of a-" a knock came at the door. They both froze.

"Kelly? Are you all right?" came Dana's muffled voice through the door. Kelly put her finger up to her mouth to signal he needed to be very quiet. She opened the door just enough to peek her head through. Any farther and Dana would have seen a lot more than she should.

"Hi, Dana! What's wrong?" she asked innocently, her eyes filled with worry.

"I thought I heard a crash down here and I just came down to make sure everything was okay," she said. Her voice was genuine with concern.

"Oh, I just dropped a glass. I'm sorry to do this to you, but I was just about to take a shower. I'm not exactly…decent," she said, feeling slightly bad at the deception.

"I'm sorry for bothering you. Just after what happened earlier, I've been nervous," she apologized, confused.

"Oh, it's all right! If I were in your shoes I probably would have come down, too. Thank you for being concerned, by the way. Now if you don't mind…"

"Of course. I'm really sorry."

"I'll talk to you later then. Bye." She closed the door before Dana could reply. They waited to hear her neighbor go up the stairs before speaking again.

"Nice lie," Hawk laughed.

"Thanks," she answered innocently, as she turned back towards the boys. Hawk had taken the quilt off of Snap, just as she was about to do.

"Is Will gonna be OK?" Jax asked, appearing in the doorway.

"Yeah. He's going to be just fine. Don't worry," answered Kelly with fake cheerfulness. Jax looked at Hawk for reassurance.

"He'll be fine, Kid," said Hawk without any of the usual edge in his voice.

"Then can I take a shower?"

"Of course, Jax. Use the upstairs bathroom—you'll have more privacy and that's where everything is anyway."

"Okay. Plus then that lady'll hear the water and will think you were telling the truth." He went into the kitchen.

"He's really nine?" asked Kelly, watching after him.

"Yep. Turns ten in October."

"Amazing."

"What?"

"He's been here since he was five, so he's been on the street's since then?" He nodded in affirmation. "So then, I know that he had Snap and everything, but even he was only twelve when they started off, right? How did they make it? I know never could have. And to still be such a good kid?"

"My brother and I helped. We all do," he said, not going into any trouble to explain who 'we' referred to. "We gave them money and food and shit when they needed it. I still do, but Snap's been wanting it less and less. I think it's cause he knows I dun have a lot either – my bro was the one wit the job. No record."

"Where did he go, if you don't mind me asking?"

"Prison. Ghost is his name. Assault charges. He got…carried up in the moment."

"How old is he?" asked Kelly cautiously.

"Twenty-two."

"How old are you then? I thought you were at least that old," she knew better. It was just his presence that made him seem that old.

Hawk almost smiled. He knew she knew better, but he humored her. "Nineteen."

"What was that lady talkin' about before? Something that happened earlier?" asked Hawk curiously after a few moments of uncomfortable silence.

"My purse was taken. No big deal," Kelly said honestly not caring. She checked Snap's wounds again and changed the bandage on his leg. It was slowing down a great deal. She put extra pressure on it, trying to stop it completely. She was starting to worry about too much blood loss.

"No big deal? If you saw him, I might know who it is. I could get it back for ya. No trouble."

She let out a nervous chuckle, how exactly would he get it back? But she knew he would never do anything to the kid lying limp on the couch. "Well there's a hitch in that plan. I already *got* my purse back. And I know exactly who took it," she said. She nodded towards the boy on the couch.

"He's a good kid," sighed Hawk after a minute or so of contemplation. It was the first time she saw compassion in his eyes. "Sometimes he has to do things. He doesn't let Jax start in on it, though. He's got alotta values. More than me or Dawg do put together."

Kelly nodded and looked at the boy standing next to her. She had noticed his eyes before as shadows, nothing in them, but now she saw a lot. They looked wise to her. She wondered why—what had he seen or done? "I already know he's a good kid. It was on the front steps even before I got home, untouched except for a few dollars. There was even a little note."

All the words had barely left her mouth when there was another groan beside her. The boy's eyes flittered open. Hawk rushed to the edge of the couch, as did Mad Dawg who had apparently been standing unseen in the doorway. He whispered something to them, then closed his eyes and went back to sleep.

Kelly hadn't heard what he had said; he had said it so weakly that the boys had even heard. But they had heard because as soon as his eyes had closed again they snapped into action. They were inching to the door.

"Where are you going?" she asked them cautiously. *Do you really want to know?*

"Don't worry about it," answered Hawk. Then he turned to Mad Dawg. "You thinkin' what I'm thinkin'?"

"Yessir." Mad Dawg sideswiped his jacket to show Hawk something unseen to Kelly, but she understood. She froze. Hawk nodded soberly. *Why did I let them into my house? What have I started?*

"I thought so. You're the ones who always hang out under the light!"

"Yes, ma'am," Mad Dawg answered truthfully. "The Jokers. Protecting our neighborhood and friends for sixteen years now."

"Shut up!" exclaimed Hawk, a little more forcefully than he'd meant. He was again the kid that Kelly was scared of. "Look, we have to go take care of this. If he does this to kids like Snap, and he has goons chase little kids like Jax, he has to be dealt with." Even though Kelly didn't know who "he" was and could only assume "his" name was the one whispered, and this scared Kelly more than she had ever been, she understood. She didn't like what their way of "dealing with" something could possibly be, in any shape or form that she could think of, but she understood where they were coming from. A voice screamed in the back of her mind to call the police, but she found herself just nodding as the boys went for the door.

"Try to talk to him first. I know what he's done is horrible, but try not to hurt anyone. Anyway, I don't want to have to patch any of you up next," she half joked uneasily.

"We always do, ma'am."

6

An hour later Jax came downstairs from taking a shower. To Kelly, he looked like a whole new kid. His face was clean and he didn't look as tan as he had before. His hair was lighter than before; it was dirty blonde hair, not dark brown, as it had seemed. The only thing that was the same was his clothes. But she had an idea about that.

"What size are you?" she asked.

"Huh?"

"Clothes. What size shirts and pants do you wear?"

"I dunno. I just wear whatever they give me."

"All right. Here's what I'm going to do. I bet you I can find you something of my husband's to wear. For now. Then I'll take you out and buy you some nicer clothes. How would you like that? Whatever you want. All yours." A smile spread across Jax's face. He couldn't remember the last time he went shopping for clothes—had he ever?

"What about Will?" asked Jax, his smile fading. A worried look shadowed his young face. He glanced at his brother lying on the couch. Kelly sighed. What would she do with him? She couldn't leave him. Not now. Not like this. By now all of the bleeding had stopped, but he had lost so much blood, she didn't dare leave him. Besides, what if he woke up again?

"Well, we could always wait 'til he wakes up. I'm sure I could find something of John's that you could wear until then. Or we could wait until Hawk and Mad Dawg get back. Then they could watch him, or take you," she suggested.

"Let's wait for Will. I wanna be here when he wakes up. He might get confused if he wakes up and no one's here. You know, being in a strange place and all. I could even stay over night if he's not up yet?" Jax looked up at her with his large almond-shaped eyes. Kelly smiled and nodded gently. She wouldn't have it any other way.

"I think that's a great idea. We don't want him to be scared when he wakes up."

"Scared? Will? No way! He doesn't get scared. Nuh-uh, never." Once again he looked up at her with those big eyes, now filled with admiration. A small chuckle escaped her mouth.

"Of course not, what was I thinking."

"That's all right. I don't think he minded," he said with a worried but playful look in his eyes.

"Come on, let's see if we can find something for you to wear."

"Okay."

Then Kelly led Jax, hand-in-hand, upstairs into the bedroom. They searched through three boxes, and at every one she rolled her eyes at her husbands labeling skills. Finally they found a box full of sweatshirts and hats. While Jax was looking through that box, she found his t-shirts. When she turned back to Jax, he had lined up all the sweatshirts and hats he liked. She, in turn, did the same to the smallest t-shirts.

Kid Jax went through everything one by one. He held them up to his chest to see how big they were, looked them up and down checking for holes, and then went on to the next one. He ended up picking the very last sweatshirt he looked at. It was at least five sizes too big, but he didn't seem to mind. It was a thin olive-green sweatshirt that said 'US Marines' in large white letters. Then he went to the t-shirts and picked a plain black muscle shirt. Then as he moved to the hats, instantly gravitating to a red baseball cap with the initials USMC-452 and put it on his head. Then he changed into the black T. It hung to his knees and was not even close to hugging his body, but he seemed happy in it.

"It's too hot for a sweatshirt today. In here it's just right, but it's definitely too hot outside. Maybe tonight," commented Jax with a deep scowl. Kelly nodded and agreed with the same scowl.

Kelly thought Jax looked very odd in his over-sized shirt, old worn-out pants, and hat. She wished she could think of somewhere very close…she remembered Dana pointing out a small clothes shop down the block. She wondered if they had children's clothing. She wondered if there was enough time.

Snap had just woken up, but that was the first time since he had gotten there hours earlier. And even then it had only been for a few seconds.

"Do you want me to take you across the street and get a new pair of jeans? I promise your brother won't wake up before we get back. It'll only take a few minutes." He looked very guilty when he nodded in agreement. She tossed him a pair of her flip-flops, guessing that they would fit better than anything of her husband's.

Kid Jax looked at himself through the mirror on the closet door. He apparently thought he looked a bit weird, too, because he made a face at the sight.

Kelly checked on Snap once more before they left (everything seemed in check). They found the shop again in a hurry, and were happy to find the children's clothes up front. She let him go through the racks himself, letting herself wander over to the women's section. After all this time without a motherly-figure she didn't want to seem like too much of one. *Not yet anyway. Whoa, where did that come from? I barely know the kid.* After a few minutes he came back with two pairs of pants, a t-shirt and something in a plastic package.

"Can I get these?" he asked, holding the package up.

"That depends, what is it?"

"Boxers. I've never had them before and they're what Will and Hawk and Mad Dawg has," he answered. Kelly almost burst out laughing, but caught herself and only smiled.

"Sure. Why don't you try the pants and shirt on before we go? That way we won't have to come back later. Plus, then we'll be sure those boxers fit."

"All right." Within five minutes Jax was out of the dressing room. He confirmed that they fit. Kelly suggested getting more than one pair of boxers as well, which seemed to make Jax happy.

As they approached the cash register, Kelly was uncomfortably aware of the employee looking them up and down. It was obviously the man could see right through the oversized clothes. He politely put the clothes in a bag, but was sure to check thoroughly for counterfeit money before giving it to them. When they left and she could feel his eyes digging into the back of her head.

Even as they walked in the door and Kelly glanced to make sure Snap was still there and breathing, the phone was ringing. She left Jax to change into his new clothes and ran into the kitchen where the only phone was hooked up. On the other end was John. She quickly summarized the day's happenings, sly the information about Hawk and Mad Dawg having guns and going to find some unknown man and the total severity of Will's injuries. John was overwhelmed by this new information.

"Are you sure you're OK there by yourself? Do you want me to see if I can come home? If I explained the situation I'm sure-"

"What? Um, excuse me, sir. Could I get a leave of absence? You see, my wife befriended a homeless boy and two hoodlums and the boy's brother is in a coma now on my couch. I'm sure that would go over well." She chuckled. "Don't worry about me. I'll be fine. I have the boys to protect me."

"That's what I'm afraid of," he mumbled so he thought she couldn't hear. "I don't know. I mean, I guess if you trust them…and the one is unconscious on the couch, so he can't do anything. Just don't get too attached to them, okay? We're going to have to turn them in as soon as he's better. You know that."

"I know. Thank you, honey." A beep sounded in the earpiece.

"Hold on a second, we have another call." She switched lines. "Hello?"

"Kel! Hey, it's me, Jim!"

"Jimmy, how are you? I've missed you little brother. Where are you these days? On the farm?"

"I'm good! Still a little amazed that I got out of college in one piece, but you know – it's weird, though, they call this the real world, but it seems pretty surreal to me. But anyway, the reason I called you was because I'm *not* back home – I'm in the city and I was thinking I'd come visit."

"Oh! That would be – Oh. Err…I don't know. The house is a mess and I'm still unpacking. Maybe we could get together somewhere else or some other time…?"

"Oh, um, well," he answered dejectedly. He went on, but Kelly was distracted by the appearance of Jax.

"What do you think?" he asked with his bright blue eyes shining.

"Oh, you look so handsome in that!" she whispered quietly, trying not to let her brother hear.

"Who's that?" Jim asked suspiciously. From the tone in his voice, Kelly could tell he thought she was up to no good. Which wasn't completely off.

"Just a neighborhood kid." Then she turned to Jax and winked. "Why don't you go back in the living room with your brother?"

"OK."

Jim started speaking again. "Is that why you don't want me to come over? Because there are kids there?"

"Well, it's a little more complicated than that. How long are you going to be here? Maybe you could come over in a couple of days. Until then I'd rather not leave them alone or anything. I'm…baby-sitting…kind of."

"Well I don't…" Kelly didn't hear the rest of the sentence. Over it came the voice of Kid Jax.

"Kelly! I think he's awake!"

"I have to go Jim. Call me later! Bye!" She hung up on him, leaving Jim very confused and very unhappy at his favorite sister.

After hanging up on her brother, Kelly returned to her husband. "He's awake." But before he could respond, she had hung up.

She rushed into the next room to see if what Jax had said was true. Sure enough, over 10 hours after he had arrived, Will had opened his eyes. It had to be some kind of miracle.

Now he was trying to sit up, ineffectively.

"No, be careful. You don't want your stomach to start bleeding again," she said hurriedly.

He let himself fall back down limply. It was obvious to Kelly that he was in a lot of pain, but he would never admit it in front of them. He looked at her through teary, swollen eyes.

"Who are you?" he whispered almost inaudibly. His voice was so hoarse and shaky. "Wait. You're-"

"Yeah, yeah that was me. Don't worry about it now. Just try to rest," she told him in a low whisper so Jax couldn't hear. "Is there anything you want?"

"Thirsty."

"All right. Don't try to move." She went into the kitchen to get water.

Meanwhile in the living room, Jax was talking to his brother excitedly.

"This is the lady I was talking about! With the sandwiches!"

Every part of Will's body was in pain and it hurt so bad to talk and breath and blink. He wished so bad he could get painkillers and go back to sleep – to slip into a coma…He wished Jax would stop talking to him; that he wouldn't have to show him he was okay. But at the same time he wanted to find out about the woman he had stolen from and had, in turn, saved his life.

"Isn't she so cool? She's a nurse. She made you better," Jax went on happily. Now that his brother was awake, Jax seemed to forget all his fears.

"Yeah. Clothes?" he asked as he fought to get rid of the blood that had dried on his lip. His tongue felt weird.

"Oh, my clothes? They're mine! Well, I'm wearing her husband's shirt. I think he's in the Marines. He's not here now. And he has a Marines sweatshirt. And guess what else I got!"

Will did not like the idea of his brother getting this excited about someone, no matter what they had done. It only led to attachment. And letdown.

"Boxers!" he answered excitedly. Will started to laugh, but his lungs could not bear it and he started coughing. Pain shot through his ribs and he went to touch them. That, however, was the wrong thing to do because pain shot through his entire body. He yelped in surprise.

Jax jumped back in alarm and Kelly ran in carrying the water. Snap closed his eyes and pushed his head into the armrest, but even that took so much strength. When he opened his eyes again, they screamed with pain. Kelly wished she could give him something to help, but she had nothing but aspirin, which would make it hard for him to stop bleeding if he started again.

"Jax, why don't you go into the kitchen and get something for your brother to eat? Nothing too heavy, just some mashed up cereal in milk or a banana," suggested Kelly. Silently, Jax went off into the kitchen knowing that she wanted them to be alone.

Once Jax had gone, Kelly turned to Snap. "I'm going to check your wounds, all right? I promise I'll be as gentle as I can." He nodded uncertainly and clenched his teeth.

On his stomach, Kelly was happy to see the cuts already starting to scab over, but they looked like they might be infected. When he saw them he groaned. How did this happen? How could he have been so stupid? His stupidity had caused all of this pain.

"They hurt like hell," he commented weakly to Kelly. She poked at his chest and an odd gurgle came from his throat, surprising them both.

"I think you have a broken rib or two," she said, biting her lip. She would have to wrap them up without being able to see the problem. She wondered how Dr. Quinn had done it. She moved to his face, which she held gently in her hands. He felt trapped and wanted to run as far away as he could.

"You're lucky. If they hadn't found you, you'd probably be dead now. Or in a hospital, away from Kid Jax," she said as she prodded his face gently. "What happened to your eyes? You still have pieces of glass in them, I think. Did someone throw shards in?"

He thought a few seconds, willing his mind to remember. Then he chuckled weakly. "A blur, think a bowl? I dunno."

She moved down to his leg and he began feeling very uncomfortable. Her lips turned into a pout as she looked at his ankle. She took it in her hand and pain shot up through his leg.

"I'm guessing that hurt? I think you sprained your ankle, but it should be better by the time I let you off this couch," she said with a soft smile.

He liked her smile. To take his mind off of what she was doing, his thoughts turned to his mother's smile. Weariness overtook him. Before he knew it, he was asleep.

7

"Why would they use that?"

"What?"

"A bowl." It was mid-afternoon and Snap had just woken up. When Jax had seen his older brother asleep the night before, he had thought the worst, and it had taken Kelly fifteen minutes to calm him. Now Jax was asleep upstairs on her bed. She had stayed up all night, but he could not make it another minute without sleep. He had been up all night searching, and then all day waiting, and then waiting again, all for his trusted brother.

"We were in a kitchen I think," answered Will weakly. He was very groggy and it seemed like everything hurt twice as much as before. Kelly had to turn out the lights in the room to keep his eyes from "exploding" and his head from "splitting". But he was much more aware now than he had been earlier. And his voice came easier. He was taking in his surroundings. "There were a lot of guys. Some held me down. One of them was slicin' up my stomach." He closed his eyes as tight as he could to try to push away the pain. "At some point I got away, and I ran. But I was already hurting and bleeding – they stabbed my leg when they first jumped me. I remember that part good. But they threw something and it hit my bad leg. I was on the ground quick. When I rolled back on my back I saw the thing coming, but it was too late. I don't remember anything else."

Kelly sat back in disgust. How could *anyone* do this to a mere child? *Why* would they? She examined his leg and fought to keep her question to herself, though she knew she'd lose the fight. When she was done she leaned back against the armrest. She could hear Kid Jax moving across the upstairs to the bathroom. If he had died…what would have happened to Jax?

"Why?" An odd expression crossed Snap's face. He was contemplating what he was going to answer. He had told her what they had done to him only because it might help her heal him – and the sooner she did that, the sooner he could split. But why was something a little more intimate. Then again…In the end, he figured there was nothing to lose by telling her.

"You know what I did to you?" He didn't wait for her to answer. "Well I did the same thing to this guy's sister. Only I didn't know she was his sister. I'm not stupid enough to cross Dean on purpose. Oh. I shouldn't have said his name."

"It's okay. I don't know who that is or anything. I think you might have said it earlier anyway, though."

"Oh…shit. Not everyone is so understanding about…" he paused "pickpockets. Purse snatchers." Kelly nodded in agreement, so he continued. "She told him and showed him the note, like the one I gave you. He figured out who I was. I'm more known on the streets than I would've guessed."

Even with his earlier contemplation, Will was surprised at himself for sharing so much with the stranger. If it had been anyone else, there was no way he would be talking so much; maybe not even telling them what they needed to know. What made her different? It was because Jax trusted her, he realized. The only problem was, Jax sometimes trusted too easily.

Then his stomach started to turn more than it already had been. What if she wasn't really who she said she was? So, she had saved Jax from big guys. Any half decent person would. Obviously she really was a nurse or knew something about medicine, but what if she was planning on turning them in? She could be a social worker who was planning on turning them in as soon as tonight even. But then why would she have waited until now? Just to gain their trust and then break it again? And if she wanted to, why hadn't she turned Lane in the first time they met?

Kelly noticed his uneasy look instantly. "Are you all right? Do you need something?" He simply turned his head away to face the back of the couch. No more information was going to come from him lips. She left him alone to think.

Hours later Kelly was getting dinner ready – macaroni and cheese and soup—when she heard Jax talking frantically in the living room. When she went to investigate, she saw Snap sitting up. He was wearing a pained expression and sweat was beading down his face as he looked around to find his shirt. When he couldn't find it, he cursed loudly. Then he tried to stand. After falling back on the couch twice, he managed to stand and stay up, putting all of his weight on his good leg. He held his arm across his stomach as though protecting it.

Jax was pleading with him to lie back down when Kelly came into the mix.

"Will, stop. Please stay," Jax pleaded.

"Where are you going? Lie back down. You're going to open your wounds again, and it's not going to be pretty," added Kelly sharply, surprising herself.

"Leave me alone. Just let me go, it's better for you, lady. Trust me, nothin' good can come from me being in your house. Come on, Lane. We're going. Thanks. Really. Thanks for everything, but we gotta go." With that he grabbed his brother by the arm and dragged him to the door.

"Don't leave, please. I don't know what will happen to you if you leave. You're weak. You need food. At least wait until after dinner. You've lost so much blood. Just eat something," Kelly pleaded as she followed them into the entryway. She thought seriously of tackling him, she could take him in his weakened state, but then what would she be saying about herself? How could they trust her if she did that? Besides, she was afraid of hurting him more.

"Which door?" he shouted at his brother, much more angrily than he had meant. Jax nervously pointed to the front door. He opened the door just as a boy about his age had reached for the buzzer. Mad Dawg's head spun round fast to see who had opened the door, hoping it wasn't the lady from upstairs.

As soon as Hawk saw that his friend was awake, he couldn't help but grin. Then, realizing that he was heading out, his eyes narrowed suspiciously.

"What're you doin' here?" asked Snap, but Hawk ignored him and turned to Kelly.

"What's goin' on?" he asked her.

"He doesn't trust me," answered Kelly with a grim smile. She trusted Hawk to make the correct – and final – decision for Snap.

"Are you stupid? Get the hell back inside, kid! You hear? You'll die out here, and that ain't gonna happen. We trust her, you trust her. You got that? You're alive, aren't you?" he snapped at his friend. He threatened Snap back inside the apartment with every word. So many emotions were flowing through his head that he didn't even know if what he had said made sense.

Snap knew better than to question Hawk, so he stayed quiet. He still didn't know how they knew where they were, but he didn't want to say anything. Before he knew it, Hawk had him backing through the door.

When they stepped inside the apartment, a mixture of smells hit their noses. A faint smell of something metallic itched at their noses, but only Hawk and Kelly realized what that smell was. The other smell was food – lovely, well cooked food. Something Will and Jax had not eaten fresh in a long time. At that moment, they all realized just how hungry they were. Only Jax had eaten that day, the others had been too busy. Their stomachs growled.

"Is everyone hungry?" asked Kelly cheerfully. Jax gave an enthusiastic yes, while Snap shrugged in a defeated sort of way. Both Hawk and Mad Dawg stayed silent. They weren't sure if she meant them. "How about you, boys? I figured you'd come back as long as you didn't get caught…up."

"Yeah," answered Hawk.

"Yes, ma'am," answered Mad Dawg happily.

They ate in the living room so that Snap could lie on his couch, which they had put fresh sheets over without bloodstains all over them. Trying to leave had taken a lot out of him, but the prospect of food kept him going. He ate twice as much as everyone else in about half the time. Jax was the entertainment for the night, if you could call it that, with his recounting of the search for "my missing brother." It was hard to tell if Snap cared or not, or if he was even paying attention for that matter. Every once and a while he would give a slight nod of understanding, but he did not utter a single word throughout dinner.

Kelly and Jax were in the kitchen clearing dishes. Hawk, Mad Dawg, and Snap were in the living room, talking in hushed voices. The buzzer rang. Every one of them looked towards the door like a deer in headlights.

Who could it be? It wouldn't be Dana, would it? There was no buzzer within the building; she would have knocked. Who else could it be? John? No. Social services? God no.

"Jax, take them upstairs into my room. [Buzz] Stay there until I tell you to come down. Help yourself [Buzz] to clothes, Snap. And do be careful not to hurt yourself." She waited until they were up the stairs to answer the buzzer.

"Hello?" she said cautiously through the microphone.

"Kel? Is that you? It's Jim," came the serious voice.

"Jim?! What are you doing here? I told you to call, not come," she answered frantically.

"I did call three times today! I was worried about you! That kid was yelling yesterday. Something like he's 'awake' and it was the best thing on earth."

"Oh, nothing, his brother had been taking a nap and he woke up."

"Kel, let me in. If that was all it was then how come you're not letting me in?" Kelly winced. He could see right through her. He had always been able to. Not like she was being very convincing.

"Fine. Hold on and I'll buzz you in." She ran into the kitchen and yelled up to the boys to "Stay absolutely quiet! Someone's coming inside." Then she buzzed her brother in, cursing him silently.

She opened her door and stepped aside to allow her brother to enter. She forced a smile onto her face and a broad grin formed across his. She had missed her brother so much. He was her favorite brother, the youngest and brightest of them all. She wished he hadn't come. She was so anxious that she didn't even notice he had grown a goatee. She was only faintly aware of what she was used to as well. His blonde hair, green eyes, his magnificent height.

"You look like hell. The brats keep you awake?" he laughed. Then his face turned serious as he looked about the room. "Why are there sheets on your couch?"

"The boy who was taking a nap yesterday – he wasn't feeling good, that's why he was sleeping – so I put the sheets down for him. The towel's from the younger one's bath. I haven't gotten around to cleaning up," she answered quickly. Maybe it was too quickly because he gave her one of his yeah-right-how-stupid-do-you-think-I-am looks. She picked the towel up, greatly aware of the dried blood on it, and tossed it into the bathroom. Had he noticed? "Sorry about the mess."

"This is what my dorm looked like every day for four years, don't worry about it. So, how is it here alone…without John?"

"Oh, it's okay. It gets a little lonely sometimes, but that's why I baby-sit." Good, bring the baby-sitting in and he'll think it's legit.

"Yeah, you always did like baby-sitting me. Or should I say tortu-" he was cut off by a noise upstairs. Kelly recognized it as a yelp of pain from Snap. What did Jim think it was?

His head snapped up, he of course didn't know there was anyone upstairs. He turned questioningly towards her.

"What was that?" he asked nervously. Like her, he had grown up under a bubble, so the city apparently made him a little jumpy. And that was without cries of pain in a supposedly empty house.

"The landlord upstairs. Sometimes she keeps the TV up really loud. Don't worry about it." Kelly tried to keep a straight face, while wanting to grimace. She wanted him to believe her story, but she also wanted to find out what happened. *It was probably nothing. He is not lying dead on the ground.* Thankfully, judging by the expression on his face, he had bought it. That is, at least, until a curse came from upstairs so loud it rang in their ears. This time it was Hawk. She couldn't help but curse under her breath, if Hawk had given away their hiding place, something was wrong. *Please don't be lying dead on the floor.*

Then they heard a door open, footsteps, and another door closing. *He's not dead.* Jim looked like he was ready to have a heart attack. Kelly mumbled something under her breath and darted into the kitchen and up the stairs. Jim was left alone in the living room being more confused than ever.

Kid Jax and Mad Dawg were standing in the doorway of the master bedroom. Jax looked very worried while Mad Dawg only looked wary. The bathroom door was closed. She could hear someone throwing up behind it. Her eyes darted back to Jax and Mad Dawg.

"What happened?" she asked frantically.

"I don't know. All of a sudden he let out this weird sound, like from earlier. Then he turned kinda green where he wasn't weird looking already. Hawk yelled and they ran in there. I think he got sick," whimpered Jax. "I'm real sorry. Does whoever it was know we're up here now?"

"Yeah. It's all right, though. I think it's okay if he knows." *Hopefully.* As if on cue, footsteps were headed up the stairs. Jax and Mad Dawg ducked back into the bedroom instinctively, just as Jim's head appeared.

"I know I heard a male's voice! What the hell is going on here? Tell me the truth! None of this babysitting bullshit," he yelled. Kelly winced. Her brother, though eight years younger than she, made her extremely nervous when he was mad.

"Hey! Don't talk to Kelly like that! Where do you get off-" started Mad Dawg, stepping out from behind the door. Kelly put up a hand and silenced him. Jim froze and turned pale. He was *really* confused. He had expected an older male, maybe a lover, but a kid younger than himself?

"Jim, this is Mad Dawg. Don't let the name fool you, though. He's a very sweet kid. Jax, come on out." Jax inched slowly out of the room, taking refuge behind Dawg and only peaking his head out into view. "This is Kid Jax. In there [she pointed at the bathroom] is Snap and Hawk. Um, Snap isn't feeling too well today." Mad Dawg burst out laughing.

"Sorry ma'am. Just a little understatement," he explained after clearing his throat. Jim looked at her suspiciously. They heard a faint knock downstairs. Kelly groaned.

"What is it with talking to me today?" As she realized it had to be Dana, an idea dawned on her. "Jim, come down with me. Trust me. You too Jax, but I'm going to call you Lane, okay? Now whenever she sees you she'll have a reason for you being here." They both nodded and followed her downstairs. Mad Dawg went back into the bedroom and awaited orders.

Downstairs Kelly opened the door—all of the way. Dana stood just beyond the doorway with a worried expression on her face. When she saw her safe, a look of relief swept over her.

"Hi Dana! I'm sorry about the racket. My brother and my nephews came to visit," she explained. She continued, "This is Jim, my brother, and this is Lane. My other nephew is upstairs. He isn't feeling well."

Dana eyed the pair of boys in front of her suspiciously. "You aren't father and son. You're much too young for that."

Kelly forced a chuckle. "Of course not. Jim is my youngest brother and Lane and William are my older sister's children." Dana chuckled, too.

"Oh, I'm sorry for bothering you again. I'll leave you alone. Have a nice visit."

"Bye. Nice meeting you," called Jim as she went back up the stairs. Then they heard the bathroom door open again upstairs. Jax sprinted past them and up the stairs. When Kelly tried to follow, though, Jim held her back. He spoke in an angry whisper.

"Why am I helping these kids? After you lied? And Mad Dawg? I mean, come on! He's a gangster. Hawk and Snap sure sound like gangsters, too. Jax is probably too young to be one, but he's sure on his way. You can tell by the way he walks and how he looks up to Mad Dawg. So, why? Why them?"

"Come on, sit down and I'll explain it to you." He sat reluctantly next to her on the couch. "Last week Jax was being chased by these men, older and bigger and stronger than you. He hid in my alleyway, so I told him to come in. I hid him until they went away…and a little while after that. Anyway, I found out that he and his brother, Snap, are homeless. They've lived alone on the streets for years. I still don't know what happened to their parents. Anyway, early yesterday morning the buzzer went off. It was all four of them. I had never met anyone besides Jax before. The older boys were carrying Snap. He had been beaten up. Badly. That's why Mad Dawg laughed before. They brought him to me because they knew I could be trusted, since I'm a nurse and I had helped Jax before. If they get turned into foster care they could be split up. Hawk and Mad Dawg? They are part of a gang. I won't lie to you. The Jokers. I get the feeling Hawk is the leader. But they seem like good enough kids." Jim rolled his eyes and looked like he was on the verge of a maniacal laugh. "I think if it hadn't been for Jax and Snap they might be as bad as the rest of them, but they have big hearts believe it or not. Don't give me that look. They care about them. And they all trust me. Kind of. I can't break that trust."

"How do you know they're not dangerous? You said it yourself: you only met them today."

"They are dangerous. I already know that – I see it. Just not to me. Did you hear Mad Dawg when you yelled at me? They like me, or at least respect me. They wouldn't do anything to me. I hold that to my grave -"

"Unless they're the ones who put you in your grave."

"Besides," she continued, ignoring her brother, "Jax would never hurt anybody, and Snap only if his or his brother's life depended on it."

"Well, I still don't trust them. And if I don't see anything that changes my mind, I'm calling someone myself."

"Fine, but I guarantee that when you see Snap, you'll change your mind." She called to the boys, who had been standing nervously by the top of the stairs, listening.

First came Jax. Jim noticed for the first time just how skinny he was. He looked so fragile, like glass, and for a second he thought if he were touched he might break. Next came Hawk. If Jax was glass, then this boy was brick. Hawk was tan, about the same shade as Jax, but without the unhealthy, over-exposed look. His tan looked very natural, maybe he was Latino or had mixed blood. He only looked a couple of years younger than him, but at least a foot shorter. But still, if he met him on the street, Jim knew he would lose a fight. Mad Dawg came next. Jim realized that he was even younger than he had thought earlier, probably still in high school even. He was much taller than Hawk and Kelly, but only came up to Jim's shoulders. Everything on him was coffee-colored. His eyes, his hair, his skin. Jim could tell from the way he walked that he wasn't from the city. Once upon a time, he was from some small town, where he had been a respected, well-rounded kid.

Last came "Snap". Jim's stomach lurched. He watched as Will made his way, agonizing step by agonizing step. He was black and blue and green in the face. Jim could tell this boy was only high-school aged, around the same age as Mad Dawg, or younger, but his straight face and blank eyes gave the impression of a much older, disciplined man. He had not changed his pants and Jim could see the tears and blood. He limped badly. He didn't make any sudden movements. He was skinnier than Jax.

"So you're Snap," Jim said coolly. The boy eyed him suspiciously and he wondered if he was from social services. But he seemed too young. He wished he had been paying attention when Jax had come back up. His stomach turned uneasily.

"You're young. Who are you?" he asked in a very threatening tone. Jim remained calm.

"This is my baby brother Jim. We were on the phone when you woke up, he heard Jax and thought something might be wrong. Don't worry, he won't turn you in," Kelly answered for her brother and she stole a quick glance at him. Jim felt himself blush. *Great, show your weaknesses. If Kelly weren't here right now, they would take you out.*

"How do you know? Did he say that, or did you? How can we trust him?" The boy shot him a look of poison.

"Look, you can trust me. You have my word," Jim answered in defense of his sister's word. *Well that was stupid. No turning back now.* Snap still turned to Hawk, looking for a backing, and though his face was hard, Kelly could see a strand of doubt.

"Man, just trust him. Ya have to start sometime," spat Hawk. He turned to Kelly without any expression on his face. His eyes, though, held a secret pleading.

"You know what happened last time." He whispered forcefully, so that only Hawk heard perfectly.

Jim jumped to prove himself; he had never had his word questioned before. "You know, I'm still young. I can't be much older then you – look at me. It's not like the system would take me seriously, anyway. And I would *never* betray my sister like that. Or you. You can trust me. You have to trust me," he finished.

Snap's face hardened as he tried to think. He wanted to trust him. He wanted to trust all of them, but he couldn't. He made his voice sound like daggers – and aimed them into Jim's skin. "I don't have to do nothing! I don't have to take any stupid lies from you *or* your sister. Maybe you really don't want to turn us in, but how can I be sure? It's not only me I have to look out for, it's Jax, too." His eyes flicked angrily from one face to the other. Never once did he make eye contact.

"Kelly, ya mind if him an' me have a...chat in the other room? It's important," Hawk asked, looking at her with very weary eyes that she knew were filled with lies and deceit. *But they're not aimed at me.* Kelly nodded.

Kelly, Mad Dawg, Jim, and Kid Jax sat awkwardly in the kitchen for a long time. They tried not to listen to the heated voices in the next room. Finally, abruptly, they stopped. When they came back in, Snap looked pale under his bruising, and Hawk seemed triumphant, wearing a small, mischievous smirk. Kelly held back a sigh of relief.

51

"Well then, who's staying over tonight?" she asked cheerfully. Jax, who had been quiet until now, shouted 'ME.'

"Snap, too," said Hawk. He looked hard at his friend to make sure he agreed. "But, me and Mad Dawg have to get goin'. He's got school. Flunked math. I'm checking in with the guys, anyway. See if anything happened."

"I should go, too, sis, apparently you don't have anymore room at the inn, and I don't want to get to the hotel too late," explained Jim, then pulled her to the side. "You sure you'll be all right? I don't want to leave you alone. I really, really don't." Kelly nodded and they hugged awkwardly. She watched him go out. She knew he wouldn't call anyone.

Hawk and Mad Dawg said goodbye then, and she went to "show them out." As soon as they were out of earshot, she stopped them. From the look on her face, Hawk knew it was important.

"Did you do it?" she asked gravely. Her voice shook. They all knew what she was referring to.

"Naw, ma'am. No one was there. They must've moved or something. We will get them, though ma'am. Don't you worry about that, if that's what you were worried about in the first place." Hawk nodded in agreement, even though he knew that's not what she had been worried about.

Some time later Kelly was tucking Jax in bed (actually a mattress that she had thrown sheets and a pillow on). His brother was downstairs in the living room. There was no way he would fall asleep in this house again. No way.

Kelly walked in and gave him a disapproving look. He glared back at her. Her swagger told him she was tired, like he was. Even so, he wouldn't fall asleep.

"You really should try to get some sleep you know. You're still weak. That's why you got sick. Too much too soon." He ignored her. "I have a mattress set up in the room next to Jax's. It's not the best, but…"

"I don't take charity. I wouldn't be here if it weren't for Hawk. Otherwise I'd be gone right now."

"I don't doubt that. But, I still think you should get some sleep. It's upstairs if you get tired. I'm going to bed, though. Good night." He didn't answer.

She had been laying in bed a long time before she heard him coming up the stairs. She knew he had come out of sheer exhaustion. He had probably already fallen asleep once. He had been half asleep when she was talking to him. There was no doubt that he would be sleeping late again the next morning. Through the wall, she could hear Jax snoring.

8

The sun was rising when Kelly awoke the next morning. Though she lay in bed for over an hour, she knew there was no way she would fall back asleep. Eventually she forced herself out of bed and wandered to the boys' bedrooms to check on them. She peaked into Jax's room and smiled. There was a lump under his blankets where he was curled up.

Kelly couldn't resist going to the sleeping child. Kneeling next to the mattress, she gently pushed the blanket back to uncover the boy's face. He wasn't there. It was just a lump of tangled sheets. Panic filled her mind. They wouldn't have left. Not after what Hawk had said. What had he said?

Before she knew what she was doing, she was running to the other room. She stopped abruptly in the doorway, relief flowing through her. A smile slowly formed across her face. Snap lay under the covers. He looked, for the first time since they had met, peaceful. Even when he had been unconscious he had a sort of tenseness about him. Now though, he seemed calmer…younger.

Next to him, lying on the top of the blankets, was Jax. He was snuggled closely to his brother, like a child and mother might be. Though she doubted either knew this, his arm lay across Jax protectively. She had never seen a closer set of siblings before. But then again, she had never before met siblings who didn't have anything besides each other.

In his sleep, Jax stirred. Kelly took this as a sign to go downstairs. The last thing she wanted to do was embarrass Jax by letting him know she had been watching them.

After putting on a pot of coffee, Kelly went into the living room to relax. Soon, she had fallen back asleep (now that she was out of bed, of course). She awoke to the sound of feet coming down the stairs. A few moments later a tired-looking Jax came into the room, rubbing his eyes. He was clad in an oversized pair of flannels and t-shirt (both courtesy of John).

"Good morning," he yawned as if he had known her for years. He shuffled over to the couch and sat next to his friend. Kelly turned the TV on and found cartoons. Kid Jax smiled and leaned against the armrest.

"What do you want for breakfast?" Kelly asked her young companion. With his wide eyes kept on the TV, he shrugged. She got up and headed into the kitchen.

Meanwhile, upstairs Will had just woken. It was quiet in the room besides the occasional sound of cars passing by below on the street. His head pounded and when he tried to get up he felt very lightheaded. His eyes were so swollen that he could barely open them. Worst of all, he couldn't remember where he was. His mind had completely fogged.

"Where am I? Why can't I remember! I know that I was here last night and I was mad. Why though?" he muttered to himself. The last thing he could clearly remember was being at his building…and then nothing clear.

He looked around, trying to remember something. His eyes were teary and they burned badly, but he still saw it, the sweatshirt he had taken from a box. It had been too hot to wear it. In the middle of the night he had woken up and Jax had been there. He said he couldn't sleep so he climbed in bed. He had taken it off then. Whose was it, though?

Kelly's husband. He winced at the realization. He hadn't trusted her, that's why he had been mad. He still didn't. This lady had to want something. No one takes homeless kids off the street without turning them in or doing something worse. He had learned that the hard way.

Jim. Hawk and Mad Dawg. Dean. Everything rushed back quickly. The fight came back in one big chunk. He now remembered it better than he had the day before. Everything about it pushed at him. The man standing over him with the knife that had been centimeters from his throat – it made him numb just thinking about it. What had made them stop? He pushed the memories into the back of his mind and put all his energy into getting up.

After trying twice and failing, he finally managed to sit up. He put his hand against the wall for support. His legs felt weak and wobbled under him. The room seemed to be off balance, like it was teetering on the edge of a cliff. Pain blurred his vision worse as he put weight on his leg. In his stomach acids turned, making him feel sick, but wanting food at the same time. It was as though his body didn't want him to stand. It wanted him to give.

At the same time, Kelly had decided to change out of her pajamas. As she walked past Snap's door, she glanced in on him. He was sitting up, trying to

54

stand, but without much prevail. He seemed to be in worse condition than the day before. He was breathing very heavily.

"Do you need any help?" asked Kelly.

His head shot up to look at her, sending pain up his neck. If she hadn't spoken, he never would have known she was there. His eyes were tearing so badly now that she almost blended in with the rest of the room. Nothing had it's own definitive shape anymore.

"No," he snarled. *But she's a nurse.* Just as she turned to leave, he spoke again, a bit easier this time. "It just hurts. A lot. And I can barely see."

"I'll be right back. Lay back down." He obeyed and closed his eyes. Only seconds passed before she came back holding a mini flashlight.

"All right. Open your eyes." Will obeyed and looked up at her. She was at the edge of the mattress. She looked like a dark shadow.

A light turned on in front of his eyes. It shone in his right eye first, then his left. It hurt so bad. His eyes burned, and he fought to keep them open. He could feel tears trickling down his face. The light triggered his headache and made it three times worse. If the light didn't turn off soon he would be sick.

The light turned off, and he heard the sound of Kelly putting it on the ground. Then she put her hand on his knee. She sighed. He tensed.

"It looks like you still have some shards of glass stuck in your eyes that got irritated. We'll try to wash them out." She led him to the bathroom and filled a mini cup. She told him how to wash them, then allowed him to do it himself.

"How's your head?" She asked as he leaned his head back.

"It hurts like Hell." He took his free hand and pressed it against his forehead. The pain didn't ease. She was silent while he switched eyes.

"I think you have a mild concussion. You should be okay, now."

He now stood with his eyes closed. They felt better now, but he was afraid that when they opened they would hurt just as bad.

"So I'll be okay?" he asked and opened his eyes. They were still sore, but nothing like before. He could see a little better.

"You should be in a few days or so. You need to take it easy though," she answered. She went to put her hand on his shoulder, comfortingly, but he moved away. He would not get close to this woman. He felt her hand gently on top of his, but he snapped it away. There was no way he would get close to this woman. Even if Jax trusted her, he couldn't. He knew more about trust than Kid Jax ever could.

"Can I go back to sleep now?"

"If you want to, but I'm making breakfast soon." His stomach turned and grumbled at the same time.

"Oh. I'll come down, then." He wondered if he would throw it up again. "You want any help?"

"No," he answered quickly and sharply. *It's better if she thinks I don't like her. What the Hell am I saying?! I don't like her.*

Downstairs Jax had been watching the cartoons in amazement. Never could he remember a time seeing anything better. Of course, he hadn't really watched TV since he was five, in an ancient time that he could barely remember anymore. Once and awhile he would watch the news or sports through a store window, but there had never been sound and it had never been "chock-full of adventure" like this was.

He was so mesmerized by it, he didn't even notice when his brother entered the room until he passed in front of him, blocking out the picture. He sat down next to his brother. Without turning his head from the screen, Jax leaned against the older boy's side. Will winced, but let him stay.

"What are you watching?" he asked, even though he already knew the answer – it had once been his own favorite cartoon.

"The Smurfs. It's about these mini blue people things. Then there's this cat and a old guy and they're bad guys," he responded. He glanced a second at his brother.

"Ooh yeah, that used to be my favorite Saturday cartoon. Except, I watched it on Wednesdays."

"You've seen this before?!" exclaimed Jax in excitement.

"Sure. So have you. You used to watch it with me all the time. You were only two at the time, but still. I guess I was your age when we watched it."

Kelly poked her head in and announced that she was making eggs, bacon, and toast. Will's mouth practically watered. He missed all those breakfast foods. Too bad he would be leaving soon. Despite that, his lips curled into a smile…but not long enough for her to see it. Jax thought momentarily about how he had wanted bacon so badly the day he had met Kelly, then his thoughts went back to the show. Kelly disappeared back around the corner.

"What about Hannah?"

"What about her?" Will was taken off guard and tried to seem calm, but his voice shook anyway.

"Did she watch it?"

"Oh…uh…Yeah, she watched too. We all liked it."

Kelly, who had been getting a pan from just inside the kitchen door stopped. *Who's Hannah?*

9

Later that day Jim called and told Kelly that he would come over later for dinner, and he would be supplying the food. So, as morning gave way to afternoon, Will decided to take a shower. The last shower he had taken had been days earlier. He figured it was about time. *I probably smell like crap.*

Though it looked smooth and stringy, his hair was snarly and he could barely put a brush through it. It seemed to him that the more he brushed, the worse it got. Eventually he gave up and shampooed it. He was happy to find that when the oily conditioner was in, he could brush his hair out easily. No afro today.

By the time he got to soap up, he was very tired and he thought his leg would give out any moment. However when he went to sit, he discovered the ground water was very dark from dirt and blood, so he leaned against the wall instead. He rubbed hard, trying to get all of the grime and filth off. His cuts stung like he imagined killer bees would. The water slowly turned clear. He got out.

With a towel wrapped about him, he went to the sink. He could see clearly now. He could see his clean face, but fuzz was growing on his chin, showing signs of age. *Where did it all go?* He realized that he hadn't shaved in a couple of days. Usually he had a stash of razors somewhere, but being here didn't make it easy for him to get them. If they hadn't been stolen.

He studied his teeth. Lucky for them, one of the Joker's moms was a clean teeth freak. He always had extra toothpaste and toothbrushes lying around the house. The hard part was getting them out of the house without her radar going off. Not that his teeth were healthy looking. His not eating took their toll on them. But though they did not look particularly good, they weren't horrible either.

The swelling on his face had gone down a great deal since the day before, according to Kelly, anyway. Even so, as Jax put it, his head was bigger than usual. Both of his eyes were black and shiny and puffy. A long bruise ran from the top to the bottom of his left cheekbone. There was a large bruise covering his right cheek. His lips were cut and a sore had appeared in the front of his mouth. His tongue still felt very weird.

"What did you get yourself into? You should've stayed," he mumbled to himself. *No. Then we'd all be split up. They'd be adopted...in different houses. And I'd be in foster care. I'd be too old, not cute enough. No one would want me. At least this way Lane and I are together. And Hannah's somewhere safe.*

Turning around to where he had left his clothes, he found they were gone. Lying in their stead was a new pair of jeans, a Billabong t-shirt, boxers with a weird, square, yellow man, socks, and sneakers. They all looked to be new, except the shoes which were probably her husband's. Putting them on, he found they all just about fit. But for some reason, the new clothes got him mad.

She doesn't have the right to get rid of my clothes and get me new things that she doesn't even know I like. But I do like them. No. It doesn't matter. I'm getting my old clothes back.

He charged out of the room to find Kelly. She was in the kitchen, talking on the phone. Jax was nowhere to be seen, *good,* but considering there was Chinese food on the counter, Will figured he and Jim were upstairs. Kelly smiled at Will, but it faded nervously.

"John, I'll call you later. Take care. I love you, too. Be careful. Bye." She hung up the phone.

"What did you do with my clothes?" There was only hate in his voice.

"They're in the wash. Why? Don't you like those?" He didn't answer. "What's wrong?"

"You had no right to touch my stuff. You should have asked me first."

"I'm sorry," answered Kelly with a sincerity that was impossible to fake. But he couldn't believe her.

"Look me in the eye and tell me," he dared. She looked at them, ready to tell him, but he knew his eyes were unreadable pits, betrayed many times and that were scarred by horrors that a sixteen year old should not have seen. That no one should see.

Though she was sincere, when she opened her mouth her eyes fell. She knew that no matter what she said he wouldn't trust her anyway. He couldn't trust her. Something had happened that prevented him from trusting anyone. "I thought so."

He turned and went through the kitchen door. She didn't try to argue or follow him. It wouldn't help. If she pushed harder, it would most likely make everything worse. She had learned that much with eight siblings. She heard the front door open.

Jim and Kid Jax came down the stairs. From the expressions on their faces, she could tell they had heard most of the conversation. Jim had a protective, and restraining, arm around Jax.

"Where's he going?" the boy asked in a desperate voice.

"I don't know," answered Kelly.

"Is he coming back?"

"Most definitely. You're here, aren't you? He'd never leave you."

"He left Hannah."

"Who's Hannah?"

But Jax had realized his mistake and closed his mouth. Kelly got out the Chinese food and they ate silently.

Will didn't know what to do. Thoughts were racing through his head non-stop. He felt guilty about not trusting Kelly, but at the same time he really didn't. After all, she couldn't look in his eyes and tell him the truth. *But no one can. Not even Hawk. No one besides Ghost can, but that's cause he has more. He has more ghosts than I do. How fitting. But it's not like I don't like these clothes. It's not like she gave me bad clothes. And if she were going to turn us in, she would have already, right? Why wait days? Why wait until I'm not dying? What the hell am I afraid of? I'm going back now.* He returned to Kelly's apartment three hours later.

Jim had left an hour earlier, after he and Kelly both tucked Kid Jax into his bed. Before he could go to sleep, she had to reassure him that his brother would be back tomorrow, if not sooner.

Though she was tired, she decided to stay up and wait for him. She didn't want to leave the door unlocked for him, just in case he didn't come in tonight, but some stranger did. She sat on the couch, watching the news. No buzzer. Then she watched the late news. Still no buzzer. She checked out the window. Sure enough, to her left she could just see him sitting on the stoop, head in hands.

She smiled sadly to herself, and then went outside. It was warm out, at least seventy degrees, and there was a light breeze.

When the door squeaked open, he jumped in his seat and turned around warily. *Don't be the lady upstairs to kick me off.* But it wasn't. It was Kelly. And she was amazed by how very old and worn he looked in the shadowy streetlight.

10

"Why didn't you buzz in?"

"I didn't wanna wake Jax up." He sounded tired. He turned back around and stared at nothing across the street. She felt that he was silently inviting her to sit beside him. She sat, leaning against the handrail, and looked up at the sky.

"You know, where I come from, you can see millions of stars. It's really depressing not being able to see them." They sat in silence for a long while.

"Before we moved here, I remember being able to see stars. Not millions, but enough on a really clear night." She was surprised at his openness.

"Where did you live?"

"Jersey. Nothin special, but it was nothing like this, either. It was urban country," he added with a smile that told her it was an inside joke of long ago.

"I've never been to New Jersey myself. Actually, I've only been in one other state besides this one. Wisconsin. My sisters and me would sit up on the roof and watch the stars. The boys would be off making mischief somewhere. The only one of them who ever watched the stars with us was Jimmy. And that was only because he was the youngest and they didn't want him tagging along when he was real little. By the time he was accepted by them, they were all in college anyway. But we would sit up there and, when we were real little, think up ways that we could catch them and put them in a jar, like fireflies."

"How many brothers and sisters do you have?" he asked with true interest. Before now, he had never particularly thought of her as a real person, with a real past. Maybe if he knew something about her...

"Four brothers. Four sisters. Danny's the oldest. Then Kristy. Then Sammy and Robbie. They're twins. I can never remember which one came first. Then me. Then Jenny. Then Livvy, Jimmy, and the baby of the family is Jill. She's a little older than you."

"Jill? Not Jilly or something stupid like that?" he asked soberly.

"No...Why would it be that?" she laughed.

"Nevermind." Another few minutes passed in awkward silence. Then he said something so surprising, Kelly figured she had heard wrong.

"What?" she asked.

"I don't not like you." He wanted to take it back. To not let her know. He fought himself for control.

Kelly looked at the young man beside her. He looked straight into her eyes, and this time she didn't look away. She smiled and a small, sad smile crept onto his face. It was the first smile he had directed at her.

She asked carefully "What would it take for you to trust me then?"

"I don't know. Just promise me you won't turn us in. We've already-" he stopped himself. Was he getting carried away? Could she be let in? His eyes looked her up and down. They studied her – searched for the answer on her body somehow. Then his eyes fell on her face – to her kind eyes. He looked across the street. "My sister's already gone."

Her whole body ran cold. "Hannah?"

He looked at her through the corner of his eye warily. "How-"

"I heard you and Jax talking about her this morning. Then he said something about her right after you left. I didn't know who she was, though."

"What did he say about her?" Fear had taken place over his wariness.

Kelly didn't know whether to tell him or not. It would hurt him to know that Jax thought he had left him. But, in the end, she realized it would be much worse if she didn't tell him now.

Slowly she answered, weighing every word. "He asked if you were coming back, and I said something like 'he wouldn't leave you.' Then he said 'but he left Hannah.' He wouldn't explain what he meant."

He turned from her then, scared of what she might see. She might see the real him. The scared, guilt-ridden little boy that only he knew existed. He knew she would see anyway, though.

Kelly realized his breathing had changed. It had gotten more erratic. His body heaved uncontrollably. He was crying. *What should I do? Comfort him.*

She put a gentle hand on his shoulder and squeezed comfortingly. This time, he didn't pull away. Instead, he drew up his breath and faced her. Tears streaked his black and blue face. He hated himself for crying. He wiped the tears away.

"It was-...it wasn't my fault. You have to understand. If I had gone back in...If I had gone back in Lane would be alone out here. He wouldn't have even made it a week. He was only five...I couldn't leave him. She could take care of herself. Besides, she told me to go!" He rambled on as if he were trying to convince the world – or himself. He had stopped crying, but his voice was hoarse and seemed about to break.

"I believe you. Snap. Please don't blame yourself. You did what you had to do," she comforted, wishing she had the whole story.

"But..." his eyes looked at her with great horror. "I should have gone in instead of her. It should have been me in there. She should've stayed with Lane. I would have been able to get back out before...Now she's somewhere...God knows where! And I'll never see her...I'll never see her again." His face hardened into a much deeper anger than what she had seen earlier. In fact, she couldn't think of a time where she had seen someone this angry, and she wondered if it was all aimed at himself. To have that much self-hatred...

Slowly, his hardened eyes gave way back to sorrow. It was a sorrow to which she was grateful to have never experienced herself. He breathed deeply, calming himself. He had already showed too much. But Kelly did not back away. She would be there if he needed her. She tried to think of something she could do, and only thought of one.

Kelly embraced him in a hug. At first his arms lay limply at his sides. Besides his brother, he could not remember the last time he was hugged. He didn't know quite what to do. He imagined her if she was his mom. He returned the hug and laid his head on her shoulder. He felt hot tears streaming down his face and hoped they would go away.

But they would not; they had been burning at his eyes for over twelve years without prevail. He hadn't cried when daddy left, even at three he had to be strong for mommy. Not when mom died, he had to be strong for Hannah. Not when they had lost Hannah, he had to be strong for Lane. The following years he had to stay strong for Lane, too, he would have died before letting it known he was scared.

For another ten minutes he cried until her t-shirt had soaked through and her shoulder was wet. Finally, his breathing returned to normal and the tears went away. He came out of the hug. His eyes were once again hardened around the edges, but in the center they were soft. Kelly had not yet seen these eyes geared towards her.

He had lived with all this guilt for so long without telling anyone. Kelly wondered if Hawk even knew about Hannah. She had so many questions, but now was not the time.

"You should get some sleep," Kelly told her young companion. He nodded and she led him back inside.

"I'll tell you the whole story another night?" Will offered. They were standing outside his door now.

"You don't have to."

"I want to." She smiled as he went into his room. They had finally made steps toward friendship tonight.

11

By the time Kelly woke up the next morning, it was well past ten. Again she found Jax's room empty, but this morning she could hear him downstairs. She could hear him talking to someone in an excited voice, except Snap was still asleep in his room. She nervously wondered to whom Jax was speaking.

Downstairs she found Jax sitting at the kitchen table talking on the telephone. Kelly was flabbergasted. Who could he be talking to?

"Oh, she's up!" Kid Jax turned and looked at her. "It's John. He's cool." Then, talking into the receiver he said, "here you go."

Kelly took the phone and Jax went into the living room to watch cartoons.

"So, what were you and Jax talking about?"

Kelly could hear marines in the background yelling cheerfully. It sounded like there was music as well as a poker game going.

"Hello to you, too. Nothing really, just small talk."

"Hello. So, do you like him?"

"He seems like a very nice kid. Maybe when I meet him Tuesday I'll get a better read on him."

"Tuesday? Where are you?"

"Yep. It went a lot smoother than we thought it would. And as to where: confidential, but I can tell you we're not in Kansas anymore, Toto. You haven't gotten attached to them, have you?"

"Well...I think we should talk."

"Kelly, they can't stay at our house," he lowered his voice. "Someone might get a little suspicious. After all, you would have been *twelve* when you had the older one – Scab or whatever. Besides, Dana knows we don't have children."

"Snap. His name is Snap. Besides, that's not exactly what I was thinking of. And, um, there might be a girl, too."

"A girl? Since when is there a girl?"

"There's been a sister, Hannah, the whole time, she's just not with them. And she's around Snap's age," she replied calmly. She hadn't meant to get him worked up.

"From zero to three kids, two of them teenagers, in a month? I'm sorry, but no way."

"We'll talk about it when you get home, all right? And don't worry, I won't do anything stupid before you get home."

"Kelly, it's just that I don't think I'm ready to start off so big. Literally." His voice had risen, but it was still quiet enough for the men in the background not to take notice.

"Please John! Just wait until you meet them. Don't say no until you meet them."

"Bu-"

"Please!"

"All right, all right. But only because I don't want to get into an argument over the phone."

"Thank you, Johnny. I love you."

"I love you, too."

"So...you're coming back Tuesday! What should we do first?" Kelly asked, blatantly trying to change the subject.

"You know what I want to do. Although I'm not so sure how that would work with two kids in the apartment."

"Oh shush. I could always send them to the store. They still have to buy clothes and shoes and manly things. Maybe I should go with them for that actually. Or maybe you could! They would probably feel more comfortable with a man, don't you think? I'm sorry. I'm going off about them again."

"It's all right, but I'm starting to get a little jealous. I take it you and Scar are getting along then?"

"Yes. Speak of the devil..." No later had she said it that he came limping down the stairs. "Good morning, Snap."

"Call me Will if you want. Just not around Hawk and Dawg...This really hurts like a...yeah...in the morning," he told her, gesturing to his body lazily. He did not seem to notice the phone in Kelly's hand, or maybe he just didn't care.

"Thank you. And I'll get you some aspirin in a minute." He shrugged and slowly made his way to the living room.

"Was that him?"

"Yep," she chuckled. "I think he finally trusts me. We had quite a chat last night."

"So I take it. What did you two talk about?"

"Oh nothing…just small talk."

"Who was she talking to?" asked Will. He and Jax sat on the living room couch, watching cartoons. Will would have rather been watching anything else, but Kid, true to his name, seemed to enjoy them, so he didn't object.

"John. I was talking to him before, too."

"Really. She let you talk to him?"

"I picked up the phone. She was asleep."

"You're not supposed to pick up other peoples phone…Did he seem nice? Do you think we can trust him? Like we trust her?"

"I don't know. I guess."

"I'm gonna let her call me Will. Do you wanna be called Lane?"

"I dunno."

Though he hated to admit it, over the course of the night, Will had come to trust Kelly a great deal. No one had ever seen him cry before. He had lowered his guard – let himself go. He had never allowed that before. Not in from of anyone: not Lane, not Hannah, not Hawk. Of all the people in the world, why had it been her? Why had it been her that he had both stolen from, and been saved by? It wall too much to be coincidence. Since the night before, Will had come to trust Kelly a great deal more than before. Though he hated to admit it, he trusted her almost as much, if not more, than Hawk. No one, before last night, had ever seen him cry. Not Lane, not Hannah, not Hawk. Of all the people in the world…why had it been her? Why was it her that he had both stolen from and been saved by. It was all too much to just be a coincidence. Maybe she was the one who was supposed to take care of them.

There were only two problems: Jim and John. Jim wouldn't trust him after what had happened last night. They hadn't even gotten along the first time they had met. But he did like Jax. Maybe that would be enough. John hadn't met either of them yet, but he and Kid Jax had spoken on the phone. Would that be enough? He doubted it. He would have to be really good when John came home, whenever that might be. He really wanted this. He liked it here. For once, he had found a place he wanted to stay.

"Hey Kelly," he called into the other room. "You want to finish that conversation we were having last night?"

"Just give me a couple of minutes," she called back, apparently still on the phone.

Jax gave him a questioning look, but Will shook his head. The boy shrugged and went on watching his show.

12

"It was about four years ago. I had just turned thirteen, which meant I was the oldest. Hannah was…is…three months younger than me. I know…that's impossible." Kelly and Will sat on the roof of the building. They were both afraid of what might happen if Dean found out he was alive, so they had decided to go where no one would see them. "We're only half related. We have the same dad. He knew mom was pregnant and he still fu-…cheated on her. Then, he had the nerve to dump Hannah with my mom when we were toddlers and ran off with the other woman. But we loved Hannah anyway. It wasn't her fault.

"Anyway, it was about four years ago-"

"Wait. Sorry, but how was Jax born then?" Kelly was already having trouble following the story.

"My mom remarried. They had Lane and we were all one big happy family. Dysfunctional, but happy. Then my mom got a new job and we moved to right outside the city. One day some maniac driver runs a red – right into my mom and Frank. The doctors said they both died instantly. Our dad was gone, our parents were dead, and no relatives, so they sent in the social workers. They told us straight out we'd probably be split up. We couldn't have that. Little Lane needed us. So we planned our escape.

"The day after the funeral we were brought back to our house one last time to collect our things. This was our only chance. The man, Mr. Fluffle, no kidding, was, what else, eating in the kitchen while he thought we were getting our stuff. We climbed down the gutter, something our mom had taught us to do in a fire, and started to run down the street; towards the city. We didn't have anything besides little backpacks filled with a change of clothes, a couple of dollars, and some food.

"Then she stopped.

"'I forgot my journal.' 'We can't go back,' I told her. She wouldn't listen though. She wrote everything in that damn journal. We argued for a long time. In the end, that's probably why she got caught; we took too long. She ended up winning, like always, and we went back. Lane and I hid behind the bushes while she went back in; she was the only one who knew where it was. Almost as soon as she was inside we heard her scream. Then she yelled to us. 'Go, Will. I'll find you.'

"I haven't seen her since."

They sat in silence for a long time. Kelly took in the story. She didn't know what to say. Will played nervously with a loose pebble, waiting for her to say something. Anything. Finally, she said something.

"I'm so sorry."

"Yeah, right."

"I'm serious."

"I know you are, but you can't say it until you know what it feels like – which I hope you never do. Having all this weight." He chose his words carefully, "It feels like you're drowning, but you never actually die. It's this constant panic, you know? You're breathing, but it's like it's not air anymore. And you wish that it would end – that you would just stop breathing in this non-existent air. But you can't stop because there are people who need you. There are people who *depend* on your survival. It sucks. Really bad."

"I know I don't know what it feels like, but I want to help. I want to help you take some of that weight off your shoulders. You don't have to be drowning anymore."

In her eyes Will knew that she meant every word that she said. Over the past three days she had gained so much love for both of them, he could see it. And even though he still didn't want to admit it, he had learned to care about her, too.

It happened in what seemed like overnight. He couldn't remember it specifically happening. Maybe it was when he had shown her his true self. Maybe it was there before he had woken up that first morning and met her. Maybe it was even there when he had taken her purse.

No, he thought, *it was after that. It was when Lane told me about her. Before I even knew who she was. It was when she helped* him.

He felt a hand on his shoulder and realized he had been sitting there for a long time. Kelly had gone and come back again without him realizing. He had never let his guard down like that before. Even last night he had had one eye and ear out for trouble. He always knew what was going on around him. Something was different now.

He felt safe.

"Come on," came her soft voice. He knew it was Kelly, but it didn't sound like her. It sounded like a voice from long ago. Whose was it? It wasn't Hannah, so who? An alarm in the back of his mind went off.

"I have to go to my building," he said suddenly, without turning around. Kelly was surprised that there was no emotion in his voice. He could feel where she was staring at the back of his head.

"You can't, who knows what will happen if-"

"I have to get pictures. That's what I was doing when I got jumped. This is the first time I thought of getting them since...Please. I have to go," he pleaded, turning to face her. "They're the only thing I have that makes me remember."

"Someone is going with you, then. Either Hawk or Mad Dawg or Jimmy. Your pick, but someone." Will nodded in agreement.

Will and Hawk had gone. Meanwhile, in the apartment, Mad Dawg and Jax were playing Sorry, which Jimmy had bought for him. He had already given in to the fact that someday these two boys would end up being something like nephews; whether he liked it or not. So he figured he may as well be Jax's favorite uncle.

Snap was a whole other story. Even though he had brought him supplies (non-girly shampoo, men's deodorant), he figured that as long as Snap stayed like he had been the last two times they had met, they would never get along. Snap was a self-absorbed gangster who would only bring Kelly grief. But as soon as he walked through the door, Jim knew he was different – for one reason. Snap was smiling. Jimmy had thought he would never see the day.

Then another thing happened that surprised Jimmy further; he went upstairs to talk to Kelly. A lot of thoughts ran through his head as he tried to figure out what he had missed. He realized he would not know until speaking with his sister, so he turned his attention back to the problem at hand: what to order for dinner.

Upstairs, Will knocked on Kelly's bedroom door. A muffled voice came through the wood that Will thought asked him who he was. He said his street name and she told him to hold on. The door opened.

"Are those them?"

"Yep."

"Can I see them?"

"Well that's why I brought them up. But before I show 'em to you, we have to get one thing straight."

"Okay."

"You can't replace my mom."

"I'm not trying to."

"All right. Then, here." He handed one of the pictures to Kelly.

It was of Will, Jax, Hannah, and who she assumed were their mom and Jax's father. It had been taken at least six years earlier. In the front row were three small children. Little Jax was two or three with dusty blonde hair and the same large grin she was used to. Will was there, too. He looked to be about ten. His face was filled with a boyish glow and a grin that spread from ear to ear. His dimples were so large you could hide in them. Kelly looked at the present day him. His smile was only half-hearted now. His dimples were nowhere to be seen, either. She figured he was too skinny to have them now. In the picture his hair was lighter brown than it was now. His eyes were hard and angry now, where in the picture they were bright and large. It was hard to imagine them being the same person. Next to him was a girl the same age. She had almost black hair that fell somewhere below her shoulders, and she had darker skin than the rest. And she had the strangest eyes Kelly had ever seen. They were beautiful. Her smile was just as big, if not bigger, than her brothers'. But even with the huge smile there was a sad essence to her, but that might have been Kelly's imagination. Unlike her brothers, she had freckles dotting her nose and cheeks.

Behind them were the adults. The mom had brown hair down to her shoulders. There was something about her smile that showed she was sweet and full of youth. It saddened Kelly to think of this vibrant young woman dying. She silently cursed the driver.

"What was her name?" she asked.

"Diane." Kelly could hear the sadness in his voice.

Next to her was a man a few years older than the woman. The present day Jax was the spitting image of him. They had the same dark brown hair, as well as eyes. They had the same smile, too. His hands were on Will's shoulders protectively. She could see the love he had for this boy who wasn't even his.

They looked like a perfect family.

Will handed her the next picture and it was of Jax when he was only a few months old. Baby Jax was sitting on a baby swing in, presumably, their backyard. Hannah and Will were in the background playing in a sandbox. It was probably autumn based on their clothes and the leaves swirling about them.

The last picture was of the two older children as toddlers – probably just after Hannah had been left behind. They were sitting on an old green love seat. They sat with their backs against opposite arms of the chair. Innocent smiles were present on both faces and they were holding out their hands as if they were reaching for each other.

They were the cutest toddlers she had ever seen. Both had little button noses and were chubby little things. No one could deny the happiness in the children's faces. Why did it all have to go?

"One question," Kelly said after she was finished studying the pictures.

"Okay," he replied.

"Why is Hannah so exotic looking?"

"I don't remember her mom, but I think my mom told me once that she's half Hawaiian, and my dad's partly Latino besides that. I think, that right now, wherever she is, guys are swooning all over her," he said, and laughed.

Jimmy and Kelly stood in the foyer. Hawk and Mad Dawg had gone hours earlier, and Kid Jax was in bed. Will was upstairs taking a shower while his clothes were in the wash.

"Well," Jimmy laughed, " I never thought it would happen, but today I became friends with two gangsters and a would-be gangster I never thought I would trust. What happened?"

"Yeah, well, he even surprised me. Honestly, I didn't think he'd ever trust me. And no offense, but I can't tell you what happened since last time you were here."

"I respect that. At least tonight I don't have to worry about leaving you alone. Take good care of them, okay? And make sure they take care of you, eh?"

"Sure," she chuckled. They hugged and he left, not noticing Dana in the shadows. The rest of the night Kelly had a light heart. Nothing could ruin the mood she was in.

The next few nights were quiet. Jimmy visited them every day, bringing dinner with him. 'It's my job to show them how to eat right.' Jimmy had even taken Jax and Will to the mall and bought them enough clothes and supplies to last them a long time. He found that the boys were like younger brothers to him. He even became somewhat protective of them.

13

Tuesday morning, however, was filled with a completely different feeling. Kelly was beyond happy. She was ecstatic. Jax didn't know what to think. He wasn't unhappy, but he was nervous about who John would turn out to be like. Would he be like Jimmy or Mad Dawg or his dad? He barely remembered what his dad was like, but Will told him again and again about him. He hoped John was like him. Jimmy was too much like another brother to be a dad. And Mad Dawg was not father material either.

Will on the other hand, was downright scared. Thoughts raced through his mind all day about John. *What if he doesn't like me? What if I don't like him? What if he kicks us out?* What if, what if, what if. He felt sick to his stomach. Nothing Kelly told him calmed him down either, and he had excess energy all day. He suggested that they unpack more, even though they had already unpacked most of it. They worked for a good hour until he twisted his bad ankle while moving a table, causing much pain for him and a lot of anxiety for Kelly. He was grounded to the couch.

John hadn't been sure what time they were coming in, so Kelly had told Jimmy not to come over, in case they had to go out and get him anyway. But the day eventually passed into night with no signs of him. At ten, a slightly worried Kelly was about to send Kid Jax to bed when they heard the outside door. Kelly ran and opened the apartment door even before John had reached it. Stunned, John stood motionless as Kelly hugged him for dear life, then they were in a long, passionate kiss.

"Eww," cried Jax before Will could stop him. Kelly and John both started laughing. Will glared at Lane. Lane glared at Will for ruining his fun. Without noticing any of the glaring, the two adults turned to face the boys. Will started to get up, but Kelly stopped him.

"Sit down Will. Stay off that ankle," she commanded sternly. He obeyed. John turned his focus to the older boy on the couch. His eyes were still black and he still had bruises on the rest of his face and arms. John vaguely wondered how much about the boy's injuries Kelly had sugarcoated.

"Sorry I can't stand. I'm Snap." Will held out his hand and John hesitated cautiously before shaking it.

"So you must be Jax," John commented as he turned to the younger boy. Jax's chest puffed up in pride and he nodded.

"That's me," he said cheerfully. "Put 'er there." He held out his hand to John who took it, trying not to laugh. *Cute kid.*

"I've heard a lot about you two," John said cheerfully. Will groaned, then looked down at his feet when he realized what he had done. John raised his eyebrows and tried not to laugh. Kelly rolled her eyes at both of them. Kid Jax giggled.

"Don't worry. I'm not holding anything against you. Starting now you have a clean slate." Will nodded in thanks.

"All right you two, time for bed. Sorry it's so early Will, but, newlyweds and all. Where're you sleeping?" asked Kelly taking on her maternal role.

"My room, I guess. You got any books I can read, though, since it's so early?" He couldn't remember the last time he had read for fun.

"In our room. Jax, help your brother." It freaked John out how much Kelly was reminding him of his own mother. She was more attached than he had thought.

Will stood up gingerly, putting all his weight on one leg and holding his stomach to unseen injuries. It was obvious he didn't want to seem weak. Despite Kelly's direction, he walked away without help from Jax.

John sat down on the couch and looked around. Everything was sinking in now and it was overwhelming. When he was away, none of this was real. He would come back and everything would be just as he had left it. But the two children he had just met were definitely real. Seeing them was a big shock to him.

"John, are you okay? You look a little pale," Kelly said cautiously. As he sat there silently, she thought about how she could have handled the situation better. She could have sent the boys upstairs so she could talk to John first. Maybe they should have met tomorrow. Will and Jax could have stayed with Jimmy.

"Yeah, I'm fine. I was just thinking. You were the one who didn't want to have children yet. Now I'm the one who's not sure about it," he answered. His eyes were glazed, and Kelly noticed a small scar through his eyebrow that she had never seen before.

"Look, when you get to know them you're going to like them. I promise. If you can't take my word for it, then take Jimmy's," she offered hopefully.

"I'll take your word for it. Where is Jimmy, anyway?" he asked, looking around at anything but her.

"He's at his hotel. Where he's staying."

"Let me get this straight: you let two stranger kids stay in our house, but you make your favorite brother stay in his own hotel? How much space do the boys take up?"

"Well, gee, I dunno. Maybe two rooms? One for each?"

"Oh yeah, I guess you're right. But you still could have offered," mumbled John in response. His brain wasn't working at the moment, so he tried again with another question. "How exactly was it that the older one—Snap?—got beat up so badly? You never told me it was bad enough that he wouldn't be healed by now."

"I don't know exactly. Like I told you—Jax, Hawk, and Mad Dawg just showed up with him. No one told me what happened. And as for how bad it is, you knew he was unconscious for awhile." Kelly wasn't sure, but she didn't think John would take it very well if he found out that Will was a thief and that a major whatever-he-is was after him.

Kelly was getting impatient. John was getting impatient. Neither of them wanted to be talking about this anymore. They both thought the other one wasn't taking enough consideration when dealing with the kids.

"One thing, though, I told Dana they're my nephews. They're supposed to be Kristy's kids."

"Yeah, fine, whatever."

"You want to go to *bed*?" she asked. Her lips curled into a smile. John perked up.

"Is it…safe?"

"Yeah."

"OK."

Will was reading a book called *The Life of a Marine* when someone stepped into his light. He didn't even have to look up to know it was his brother. Even though he didn't feel like talking, he waved for Lane to take a seat next to him. He was silent, but Will could sense what he wanted to ask.

"He likes you, don't worry," Will reassured. This seemed to make Lane happy because he left then, never saying a word. He had barely gotten through another page before Kelly and John were coming up the stairs. But instead of seeing them, he saw two others. It was the same two that haunted him every night. His stomach turned. Rather than look at them again, he slammed the door shut.

A knock at the door. He heard Kelly's voice, but it didn't completely register. His mind was in a daze; he didn't know what was going on. Thoughts raced as he curled up on his mattress. A deeper voice came this time through the door.

"Good night!" he yelled desperately. Had they even been saying that?

"What was that about?" asked John outside the door.

"I don't know," Kelly answered quietly. "He's probably just half dressed or something."

Meanwhile in his room, Will guessed he was going crazy. Every time he thought of Kelly, he saw his mom instead. He crossed the room to the small desk, which they had placed there earlier that day. The clothes that Jim had bought for him were piled on top. He fished through them until he found the light jacket with zippered pockets. He took the pictures he had shown Kelly out of the left pocket.

With them in hand, he went out onto the fire escape. He looked up at the sky. He breathed the air. His mind wandered. He thought about his mother, about Hannah, his father, Frank, Kelly, Jim, and John. Everything came so fast and so jumbled that he didn't have time to process anything.

I wonder where dad is. Is he even in the US? Is he alive? And Hannah? Is she...Mom, I miss you. Why did you have to go? We were too little; Lane didn't even know what was going on. He thought you were on vacation or something. I won't let Kelly take place of you. I won't. I can't. Jim would be a cool uncle though. No! A better friend. I don't know if John's a good father. He can't be better than Frank. I miss you, too. Why did you have to take the parkway? You knew mom didn't like it...

There was a white light all around him. Will turned around and around again, trying to see something. Anything. A feeling etched in his mind. He was alone. All alone. No one could help him. He fell to his knees, but he couldn't see or feel the floor. He let his arms lay limply at his sides. Then a voice came from before him. No, it was behind him. Now it was everywhere. The voice was familiar. He knew it. It whispered to him, but he couldn't understand. The words were just beyond his reach. Then, "Snap."

Will woke with a start. He had fallen asleep on the fire escape. The sun had risen and was heating his already tanned skin. Above him, John's head stuck out of the window. He smiled and went back inside.

John had looked tired. Will wondered what he and Kelly had been doing all night. He didn't ponder long. Soon he had come up with an explanation that he did not want to think about. In fact, it made him cringe.

Then, like a swirl of images, he remembered the dream. For a long time he stood there, trying to figure out what the voice had been saying. Who it had been. But the details soon slipped out of his memory, until only the bright light was left. He gave up and went downstairs.

14

He was the last downstairs. Kelly, Jax, and John all sat around the kitchen table. The scene reminded him of family meetings. In the old days, his mom would call the family into a room. It was usually if Hannah or him had done something bad or if they had something serious to talk about. Then, at the meeting, their parents would have stern faces and they would trick the children into confessing. If no wrong-doing had occured, they would have a discussion. Jax, being too young to take part until the very end, usually played in the background.

Without having to be told, Will sat down. Apparently, there was some tension in the air. Kelly seemed to be happy, Lane seemed worried, and John was unreadable. Now it really seemed like a family meeting.

"Last night Kelly and I were talking," sighed John. From the tone in his voice, Will made a rash realization. They hadn't been doing what he had thought. Or at least not *all* night. They had been fighting, too. "She…we…would really like…we want you to live with us. At least for a little while. If everything goes well, maybe we could even adopt you. What I'm trying to say is…do you want to?"

Instantly, Jax's eyes lit up. He looked at his big brother for affirmation. His huge pleading eyes reminded Will of a puppy dog. There was no way that he could say no. Besides, Jax was happy there. *They* were happy there. He hadn't been this happy – or felt this safe – in a long, long time. He nodded.

"Yes!" Kid Jax exclaimed. He sprang out of his chair and wrapped his arms around Kelly, then John. He ran back to Will and hugged him, too.

Will was taking out the garbage after a breakfast of pancakes and sausage. Then, also to his surprise, Kelly asked him to take out the garbage. On his way back across the foyer, he heard someone coming down the stairs. Before he could make it to the safety of the apartment, Dana saw him. At first she looked frightened, but then a smile brightened her face.

"You must be Kelly's nephew. I hope you're feeling better?"

"Uh...yeah." The boy tried to remember what story Kelly had told her. "Much better. Thank you."

"Oh dear! What happened to your face?" Her eyes widened and her mouth hung open slightly. Will almost laughed. *A bit slow on the intake, aren't we?* he thought playfully.

"I just got into a fight with...uh...guy...a kid...at my school. Well, I mean, he goes to my school. We weren't at school. It's summer," he fumbled. Usually he could come up with a good lie instantly, but he found it hard because he didn't know what she knew – or thought she knew.

"Where do you go to school?"

"Well, it's in Wisconsin, I doubt you've 'eard of it. It's called...Oliver Brush High School."

Dana looked skeptical. "Oliver Brush? That's an interesting name. Who is it named after?"

"He was the one who founded the town. Brushfield. It actually has a bunch of different towns going to it. That's another story..." He took a deep breath. The more he babbled about it, the more convincing it would be. *The less chance to ask questions. More time for someone to save me.*

After awhile, John started to wonder what was taking so long and went out to investigate. When he saw Dana, he stopped dead in his tracks. Her eyes sprang from a sweating Snap to John. She squealed like a pig, and the boys had both stifled a laugh.

"John! How are you? Why are you back so soon?"

"Uh...well, we finished early. I decided to come home now when I found out the boys were here." Dana looked to Will, only to find him gone.

"They are handsome boys. It's funny, though. They don't look a thing like Kelly. Or her brother for that matter."

"Huh? Oh, well they take more after their father's side."

"I see," she replied. "I need to go now. I have to meet my son-in-law. He is planning a surprise party for my daughter."

They said good-bye and Dana left. John found Will on the couch. His eyes told John he was worried.

"Did she believe me?" he asked. John shrugged uncertainly.

"I'm sure you did a fine job. Don't worry about it."

"Thanks for coming out. I don't know how long I could've kept it up for. Just so you know, I now go to Oliver Brush High School in Brushfield, Wisconsin. The principal's name is Mr. Belding, and my best friends are Zach, A.C., Jesse, and Kelly. I really hope she's never seen Saved by the Bell." John laughed and shook his head.

"Let's hope not."

15

Lane woke up to a sound downstairs. It had been three days since his life had changed forever. The travel alarm clock next to him told him it was 7:45 in the morning. Kelly had been teaching how to tell time along with reading and math. On this morning, Lane was very excited. He couldn't wait to find out what was in store for today. First, they had asked him and Will to live with them. Then John had taken them all out to dinner in a fancy restaurant. The waitress had even commented to Kelly on their well-behaved children.

Jax had even decided to let John and Kelly call him Lane. Now only the boys could call him Kid Jax.

After a few minutes he fell back asleep, but he was quickly woken up again. 7:52. This time it was by shouting. *Why are people yelling?!* He stuffed his head between the bed and pillow, and fell back asleep. 8:02. Another voice was yelling. It was a man's voice, but he didn't recognize it. But there was something...It was coming somewhere very nearby. It was coming from downstairs. This was not the TV!

He jumped out of bed and ran towards the door. At the top of the stairs crouched Will, white faced. Lane had thought that nothing would ever be scarier than Will's face the day after the incident, but this face was much worse. It was filled with fear and anger. Will was scary when he was like this.

"What's going on?"

"Shhh," hissed Will. He leaned forward to hear better. Jax couldn't hear what they were saying. Then:

"One of them is right here," announced a man. Will fell backwards.

"Go to Hawk's," whispered Will. Jax didn't need telling twice and took off like lightning down the fire escape.

Kelly and John, Will, and two strange men were in a standstill in the kitchen. One was stout with balding gray hair. The other was young and tall with blonde hair. Kelly and John were arm in arm, leaning against the counter. The stout man was guarding the stairway while the young one was at the door. Will was stuck between them. It was dead silent, everyone was waiting for someone else to speak. Will could take it no longer.

"What the hell is going on?!" he yelled to no one in particular. He became aware of a throbbing pain in his head. "Who are these people?!"

"Calm down William," answered the stout man in a stern voice.

"He doesn't like to be called William," interjected Kelly shakily. He noticed that there were tears in her eyes. John, too, looked worried.

"Alright, Will, where is your brother?"

"I don't know."

"It's very important that we know where he is."

"Why?!"

"So we can make sure he's safe."

"Why wouldn't he be?" he asked warily.

"Last night, two boys were shot near here. Their names were Erik Wright and Christian Monteresi. Do you know them?"

Will nodded numbly. Erik was Mad Dawg's real name, and Chris was Hawk's. They had been shot…but they couldn't have been…they're invincible. But could they have died? No! No one else could die. Then panic filled him. He had sent his brother to Hawk. He felt ready to puke.

"Don't worry, neither boy is dead, but Chris's in pretty bad shape," said the young one cautiously, seeming to sense his anxiousness. "The reason we're here is because a witness told police that the shooter had been looking for a boy named Snap – or Will. He also said he needed to finish what he had started." Will's heart was pounding. He needed to find Lane. "About the same time we received a call saying that two boys residing at this address were runaways and that one had been beaten up. One of the boy's names was Will. We put two and two together."

"Who are you?"

"We're detectives. Now…where is your brother? We have reason to believe that word of your whereabouts may have gotten out. We also believe that whoever shot your friends might still be hanging around."

They knew Jax. They wouldn't be afraid to hurt him again. Before he realized what he was doing, he was pushing through the young detective. He could hear the man following him, but didn't dare look back yet. He wanted a good head start. A block down the street, Will stole a glance back, Kelly and the older officer were getting into a car, while the younger man and John were taking chase. John was easily passing the other man.

For blocks they ran. Will could feel every wound still on his body. With every step, every breath. His legs threatened to give, and his ankle and gash stung with every step. He glanced back again. The officer was still the same distance behind, but John was gaining on him. The car that Kelly and the old man were riding in was now stuck at an intersection two blocks back. He turned the corner to Hawk's street, but then stopped so suddenly his knees buckled and almost gave out.

He could see Hawk's building clearly. He could also see Lane clearly. And he saw the man holding him clearly, too. And he definitely saw the gun pointed at his little brother's heads clearly. It was one of Dean's men. A flash of memory appeared before his eyes, the man had been there that night. He had held him down. He had laughed.

The street was empty except for an old man running into a store down the block. He didn't even glance over.

He heard his name being whispered, beckoning him to safety. The man had not noticed him. With Lane he had leverage, but with him it would all be over. He joined John behind them building anyway. The officer caught up.

"Why'd you stop?" the man asked, frowning and panting. Will tried to answer, but could not find the words. He could not admit out loud what he had done.

"We found Lane."

16

Lane's mouth had gone dry. He was on the verge of tears. He had made it to Hawk's, but there had been a man waiting for him. He had easily overtaken him. Then he had pulled out the gun. Now they were waiting. For what, Jax didn't know. The man didn't seem to care if anyone saw him. Maybe he even wanted to be seen. A long time earlier an old man had gone into a store across the street, but no one had come since then, nor had the old man left. In fact, besides sirens sometime after the old man, he had not heard or seen any signs of life in a long time.

Then there was a movement in the corner of his eye, on a rooftop down the street. Then a group of men in the shadows. He noticed a helicopter in the air.

"Why does your brother have to make everything so damn complicated," the man growled deep in his throat as he, too, noticed the people. Jax smiled inside. He had known he would come. But he wondered where the Jokers were – why hadn't it been they saved him?

The PD helicopter came close, so Jax could see the men within. One was leaning out the door holding some sort of loudspeaker. "Let the boy go and drop your weapon."

The man scoffed and said quietly to Jax: "Either they kill me, I go to jail, or Dean deals with me. I think them killing me sounds like the best out of those, eh?"

Kid was not sure if he was supposed to answer or not, so he chose to stay quiet rather than answer wrong. The man had now pulled the boy against his body and positioned himself in the mouth of an alley. His legs hurt from standing so long and he felt himself sliding down, just to be pulled back up again. He had no idea how long they had been there. The sun was directly above them. He started thinking about *his* options and tears started to run down his face. *Either I die and I never get to see Will again, or the police save me and take me away and I never get to see Will again.*

Will looked up at the sky; the sun was high now. He was sitting on the hood of the detectives' car a block and a half down and around the corner from where his brother was. He could neither see nor hear anything that mattered. He watched a large bird fly lazily in the sky. Will imagined being that bird, and looking down on his brother. His imagination took over and he saw a lifeless Lane, lying in a pool of blood under the grinning man. He shook his head.

He wished he could remember what religion he was, he would pray that his brother was safe. He hadn't prayed in a long time. He had always somehow blamed Him for everything that had happened. But he remembered vaguely his mother praying. There was a particular prayer that his mother would say. He tried to remember the words. *Something about bread and delivering us from evil. What is it?! Forget it...Dear Lord. I'm not exactly sure how this works because I haven't prayed for as long as I can remember, which is probably a sin. I guess you must be in shock, then, hearing me after all this time, but I really need you. I gave up on you a long, long time ago, but if there was ever a chance for me to start believing, it would be now. You haven't exactly dealt me the best cards, as Hawk loves to put it, but my brother's in trouble. You've already taken my parents and my sister...and most of my sanity...so I'm asking if you could spare him. He's only nine. Please. He hasn't had a chance to experience life. He hasn't been to an amusement park, yet. He can't even remember being out of this neighborhood. He didn't even remember what a Smurf was. He's had a hard enough life already, he doesn't deserve to be shot. He deserves, if he has to die, to die in his sleep in a warm bed. Something I could never give him. If we had stayed, would you have let us stay together? If we do have to be separated, then please, please, please, please, take good care of him and make sure he gets to mom and she knows that we're safe. But by the way, if he dies, I'll hate you forever. More than I do now. Even if he does live, I might not like you any better. Sorry, it's just that I trust you about as much as that bald detective...Amen.*

And then a gunshot pierced his thoughts and he was running.

17

Kid Jax figured, with his luck, he wouldn't be rescued. His thoughts turned to his death. He supposed that this meant he was not invincible, as Will had implied so many times before. Would he get a proper burial, or would he become a nameless tomb in an anonymous cemetary, where no one would ever visit? Would John and Kelly and Jim miss him? He knew Will would, but would he shed tears? He had never before. Would Hawk and Mad Dawg show up at his funeral? How about the new kid Sam? 'Too young,' the priest would say. 'He was never given a chance.' Would Hannah ever know what happened to him? Would she see his story on the news? Would she know it was him? Would he like it with his parents in heaven? No…not yet. He wouldn't like it yet. He wanted to know Kelly and John and Jimmy. Sometime later he wanted to meet Danny and Kristy and Jill and whoever the rest were. And besides that, had he done enough good to get into heaven?

And then a gun blast, and he thought he was dead. But no, he was falling forward. Then the wind was knocked out of him as the two-hundred pound man fell on top of him. Then police officers were coming from all directions. A man reached them and pulled Jax out from under the man. The shot man groaned.

"Why didn't you kill me?" the man asked an officer who was putting handcuffs on him. There was blood streaming down his arm from an unseen wound. Jax figured he was shot in the back. He stood up steadily and looked around for a familiar face. A kind-looking woman of about Kelly's age wrapped a blanket about him.

"Where's my brother?"

"He's here. We'll get him for you." She yelled something to a fellow cop. "Are you okay?"

"I'm fine."

"We're going to get you checked out by a doctor."

"For what?"

"Shock."

"I'm not in shock. I've been in shock before. This isn't it. Where's Will?"

"I'm here." Jax spun around and faced Will. He jumped into his arms. They stayed like that silently for what seemed like forever until a hand touched his shoulder. It was Kelly, she was crying, but grinning. Then he was being pushed into an ambulance with a young man whose voice he recognized from that morning. The man reassured him that Will was following them.

At the hospital they cleared Lane of shock, and they commended Will in keeping him so healthy while living on the streets, although he was small for his age and a little underweight. Will, however, had not been so lucky. The doctor told him he was still greatly malnourished, although he had already started the road to recovery at the Olsen's, and had some condition from something somewhere that he would have to take medicine for all his life, and he had some kind of ear infection. Even with all that, he was in remarkable health. None of his wounds were infected and, besides a migraine, which was understandable after the day he had, nothing particularly hurt him anymore. But he had to stay for a few days anyway. When the doctors questioned the detectives about the boys' good health after so long, the younger detective chuckled, "I guess they got by with a little help from their friends." And though Will sensed that he should know this, he couldn't remember why.

Soon they had found him a bed in the pediatric wing. He was slightly uncomfortable about sharing a room with a twelve-year old stranger. And the gown was a whole other problem. But he figured it could be worse. While he waited for the nurse to come back from finding out if Hawk and Mad Dawg were in this hospital and if so what rooms, the detectives came in to talk.

"We had to call child services," the old detective told him bluntly, brushing his hand over his bald spot.

"What about John and Kelly?"

"I don't know about my partner," offered the young man, "but I'm going to help you in any way I can. If it hadn't been for them, your little brother probably wouldn't be alive right now, and you'd be in a helluva lot worse state. Maybe you'd even be in the bed your friend's in in the ICU, or worse. So I'm on your side here."

"Yeah. Me too," gargled the older man. "But don't expect me to speak for you or nothing like that. Oh, and the nurse said to give you this." He handed Will a note with two names and room numbers on it.

"Thanks."

Three days later Hawk was finally allowed to have visitors. Will was there even before his mother. They exchanged stories for a long time. He had asked Mad Dawg about it two days earlier, but he had left the story for Hawk to tell.

Hawk and Mad Dawg had been sitting in front of Hawk's building when one of Dean's guys came up to them with a gun drawn and demanded to know where Will was because 'his debts are growing'. They had refused and pulled out their own guns. Before Hawk or Dawg could get a shot off, though, another guy emerged from the shadows and shot Hawk in the chest. Hawk's shot had gone wild and only grazed the first guy's arm. He tried to shoot Hawk again, but Dawg had jumped in front of him, taking a bullet in his leg. He had hit his head and went out. Then Sam and Frankenstein had come and scared the men away.

"What they doin' to you now?" asked Hawk as the adrenaline from the stories wore off.

"Don't know. You?"

"Doc said awhile more. I don't know how long. The bullet stuck in my ribs. I lost a lotta blood. Couldn't have been more than you, though, Superman. Didja see the scar?"

"Good news, kid. That guy who held your brother hostage, Nick Aviello, ratted Dean out. And get this- Dean's real name is Duncan Kinklebottom. But anyway, we managed to do it without needing you or your brother involved. It looks like he'll be going away for a very long time. Just thought you should know. Detectives Miles and Sharple." Will read the handwritten note twice. They wouldn't be involved. That was good. They would be together soon. And they wouldn't have to worry about Dean splitting them up, either.

18

Two months and five days later, everyone sat in court. By this time it was early autumn and Will was officially seventeen. He and Jax had been placed in the same foster home, with a family named the Wilkins'. They were there, as well. They had been nice, but they had never connected with the boys, something they had learned not to do with temporary placements.

The previous two months had gone by slower than any other in Will's memory. He had even compared it to his first two months on the streets, saying it was much worse. John and Kelly had hired a lawyer that specialized in cases dealing with child placement. The judge had to decide if John and Kelly were fit parents, even after bending the law by not turning the boys in to child services. It was not hard to convince Jim and their parents' to come and give support, and Jim was to give a statement. Hawk and Dawg even sat in the back of the courtroom, wearing nice suits and with their hair slicked back. When she had seen them dressed up, Kelly had smiled a radiantly, and had laughed when Mad Dawg complained about being itchy.

Jax had become quiet over the previous week. The tension had been getting to everyone, especially Snap who had become almost as moody as before. But their foster parents held strong and reassured them in their own way that everything would be fine, no matter what the outcome. They had even received word from Ghost, via Hawk, wishing them good luck. And everyone in the gang, from Hawk down to Sam (known as Brass now), had shown their support (think graffiti good luck cards).

The process actually seemed pretty simple. The judge would ask various people questions and then they could add something if they thought the judge had not heard everything there was to hear.

First questioned was Kelly.

"Miss Olsen, why wouldn't you bring the severely injured Will to the hospital? What could have been going through your head to think that would be a good idea?"

"When Lane first brought him to my home, he begged me not to take him there. I wasn't completely sure what I was going to do. But then after I looked at his wounds, I realized I could take care of them myself. If at anytime he had become too sick for me to take care of, I would have taken him to a hospital right away. But he did not get worse, and I wanted to keep my word to Lane. If I was going to help them, he would have to trust me…wouldn't he?"

"After you gained Lane's trust, how did you gain Will's?"

"Honestly, I'm not quite sure about that," she answered with a quick glance at Will. "No one can be completely sure what goes on in a teenager's mind…especially one as complex as his, but I was there for him. I took care of his brother when he was sick and I took care of them even when he wasn't anymore. We had this understanding that I wasn't taking his…or his mother's…job, but no matter what happened I would be there for them."

"How long did you think you were going to keep them in secret?"

"When the detectives showed up, we were planning on bringing the boys to child services that day, but they beat us to it. We had discussed it with them the day before and they had seemed to like the idea."

"'They' meaning the boys?"

"Yes."

"And what about your husband?"

"He was in favor of them living with us. He had bonded with the boys."

"One last question, how is your job hunt coming along?"

"I got accepted at St. Luke's Hospital where I'll be an O.B. nurse starting next week."

"Anything else you would like to say?"

"Um…I'd like to say that no matter what you say today, I will always love these boys. They will always be in my heart and I will always, always be there for them."

Next was John:

"Now, Mr. Olsen, you did not know about the boys originally, correct?"

"No, ma'am, I was out of state."

"And what were you doing there?"

"I was working on a project for the Marines."

"And would you be going on these *projects* a lot?"

"No, ma'am, we only average one project per year. Other than that, I work at the base outside of the city three weeks a month with one week off. But I would not be away from home during those times."

"How long do these projects usually take?"

"Anywhere between two and six weeks, usually."

"What do you think of the boys?"

"They're good kids…"

"Is that all?"

"By no means. I'd be proud to have them live in my house. I know that they would not cause any trouble. They're very bright, and they deserve the best, whatever you decide that may be."

"And you agree with everything your wife said about this subject?"

"Yes, ma'am."

"Is there anything else you would like to say?"

"…When I first met these boys, I didn't know what to make of them. The way they came to my wife and came to live in my house was, putting it mildly, strange. But the more I spoke and bonded with them, the more I liked them…even more than that."

"You can step down."

"Thank you."

Next was Jim:

"Mr. Samuels, you visited with your sister the week of the boys' arrival?"

"Yes."

"And what did you think of them?"

"I thought that Lane was a great kid, and I remember thinking that he would fit perfectly into our family. He has the same kind of energy as my brothers."

"And what about Will?"

"Well, Will took a little longer to get to know. Most of the time I was there, I don't think he knew what to think of Kelly. He wasn't quite to the trusting point until my last few days. He was still very protective. This visit I've gotten to talk to him a lot more. He's really smart. He has better problem solving skills than anyone else I know."

"As a representative of Mrs. Olsen's family, would you take in the boys to your family and take on the responsibility that comes with it, and treat them as you would your own?"

"Yes."

The judge called upon Mad Dawg next, which seemed to surprise everyone except for him. He walked up calmly:

"You are a friend of the boys, right?"

"Yes, ma'am."

"In your opinion, has Mrs. and Mr. Olsen taken care of them?"

"Yes, ma'am."

"Do you think they love the boys?"

"Yes, ma'am."

"Do you think the boys love them?"

"Yes, ma'am."

"Why do you think this?"

"They told me, ma'am."

Next, the judge then called upon someone that no one had noticed sitting in the back corner of the room. In fact, no one had seen her in weeks. Dana was called to the stand:

"How do you know the couple?"

"They live in the apartment below mine."

"When did you first know of the boys living with them?"

"I heard yelling and I went to make sure Kelly was okay."

"And was she?"

"I don't know; she would not let me in. She said she wasn't proper."

"What do you believe the yelling was?"

"I think the older boys had been fighting with her."

"You were told they were her nephews, correct?"

"Yes."

"When did you realize they were not?"

"One night I heard Kelly and her brother talking."

"So, you were snooping?"

"No. I had been in the basement and happened to overhear it."

"What did you hear?"

"Something about gangsters and a homeless boy."

"Which did you think Will was?"

"I wasn't sure."

"How did you find out?"

"Well, one day I ran into the older boy. He looked very familiar, but I couldn't place his face – he looked like he was recovering from a hit and run. I asked him how he had gotten the bruises. He told me he had gotten into a fight, but if you had seen him, that story was just not right. And besides that, he said he was from Wisconsin, but he had a distinct city accent. At first I thought he might have been one of the gangsters, but then later I realized how I had known him. He had snatched Kelly's purse her first full day in the city. He had returned it, though, with some money and a note left in it. I knew he was the homeless then. Gangsters would have held her at gunpoint and never returned anything." She glared at Hawk and Mad Dawg. John looked at Kelly with a why-didn't-you-tell-me-what-happened look. Hawk and Mad Dawg exchanged knowing glances. Will winced.

"What did you do after you found this out?"

"I figured that he had run away…"

"And?"

"I called child services."

There was a gasp from Kelly. Will gripped his chair so hard his knuckles turned white. Hawk cursed under his breath. Kid Jax could only wonder why she would do something like that.

"You didn't confront them?"

"No."

Lane was next. He fidgeted a lot under the pressure:

"How did you meet Mrs. Olsen?"

"I just met her yesterday-"

"Oh, no, no. Mrs. Kelly Olsen," laughed the judge.

"Ooh! These guys were chasing me and she let me in her building."

"What did she do after that?"

"She gave me sandwiches and stuff."

"What was your first impression of her?"

"She was nice."

"Why did you move in with her?"

"'Cause Will got hurt."

"She took care of you when he couldn't?"

"Uh-huh. And she took care of him, too."

"I see. And where do you sleep?"

"In my room."

"Do you share the room?"

"Nuh-uh. It's mine. I have a mattress – but they're gonna get a bed—and a clock and lots of blankets."

"That sounds nice."

"Yeah."

"How do you like it with them?"

"It's really cool. They brought me to restaurants and bought me clothes and stuff and let me watch TV. Like the Smurfs. And they teach me stuff too."

"Like what?"

"Like how to tell time on clocks with hands and how to read better."

"If you could, you would want to live with them?"

"Yes!"

The last to be questioned was Will. As he sat on the chair, he became aware of every bead of sweat on his body. Every movement or sound in the room. The judge looked him up and down.

"Now Will, what does that stand for?"

"I'm not completely sure, I think it was probably William, though."

"Okay Will, what is your first memory of the Olsen's home?"

"I was on the couch when I woke up. There was a blanket over me. I remember being really confused 'cause I didn't know where I was. My brother walked in and he got really excited. Then Kelly came in."

"What did you think of her?"

"She seemed nice enough."

"But?"

"I didn't really trust her."

"Why not?"

"Because I didn't trust anyone."

"How come you trust her now?"

"I…I'm not really sure. All I know is that I told her things…things I've never told anyone. Not even Hawk, my best friend. And then I trusted her with my life. It was just something in my gut."

"You trust her with your brother's life?"

"Most definitely."

"And what about Mr. Olsen?"

"Yeah. He's really cool."

"Did they provide you with everything you needed?"

"Yeah. They got us clothes, they set up rooms, they give us three meals a day, and they got us shampoo and soap and deodorant and stuff like that. I can't imagine needing anything else."

"Could you see yourself living with them in the future?"

"Most definitely."

"And if you *were* to live with them, would you help them in any way you could, if they ever needed it?"

"Yeah. They've done so much for us, how couldn't I?"

"Is there anything else you want to say?"

"Yeah. For as long as I can remember, I've been pretending to be someone I'm not. I've had to be brave when I wasn't feeling it. I've had to be strong when I was really weak. I've had to be happy when I was sad…But now I don't feel like I have to pretend anymore. When they're around, I know that I can be who I am because they accept me no matter what. I feel really comfortable around them, you know?"

"I think I do. Did you rehearse that at all?"

"Well, a little, yeah. But no one helped me if that's what you mean, that's really what I think."

"Would you say that you loved them?" Will did not answer the judge's question. "Will? Are you okay?" He had a look on his face to which no one knew how to respond. "Will?"

"Yeah…"

"Yeah? You're okay?"

"No. I mean, yes, I'm fine. But I meant yes, I guess I do love them. It's just weird…I don't remember the last time I loved someone like I loved my mom, but, I guess I love Kelly like that. It's a different kind of love, you know? I didn't even realize it…"

"Thank you, Will. You can get down, now."

19

The judge left. During the time that she was gone, Will and Lane spoke nervously with each other. Will kept reassuring his younger brother that everything would be fine, even though he wasn't completely sure himself. When Kelly and John tried to come over, he waved them off so they could not say something like 'even if she doesn't let you live with us…' and make either of them more nervous.

There were murmurs from the other people in the room as well. Mr. and Mrs. Olsen were talking to Kelly's parents, apparently sharing opinions on the whole experience. Judging by their expressions, most of their feelings seemed to be good. Hawk and Mad Dawg had moved up to talk to Jimmy. Kelly and John went into a corner and spoke quietly.

When the judge came back, everyone fell silent and went back to their seats. Her facial expression was unreadable as she sat in her chair above all others. There was a prolonged pause before she spoke.

"After hearing everything that was said today, I've come to an absolute conclusion. There is a lot of love in this room; I cannot doubt that you, Mr. and Mrs. Olsen, will make very good parents. The boys also show great love for you. Taking in a teenager and a nine-year old is probably one of the hardest things you will ever do, but I have no doubt in my mind that you will take on the challenge full force. And you will most certainly succeed. However, given the nature of this case, there will be many precautions. There will be a social worker meeting with you twice a month for the first year and then once a month after that. But, as for now, I hereby declare you fit parents. After filling out the proper forms, you can take the boys home."

Almost every person within the courtroom let out a breath they hadn't even realized they had been holding. The boys – Kelly's boys – hugged and then they turned to hug their new guardians. People started talking loudly and the judge had to rap a gavel to calm them down.

"Listen up! You must hire a tutor to catch them up with their studies, which should prove very difficult, but they seem to be smart boys, they found you after all."

"Oh, wow, that's easy. I was afraid you were going to say something that we couldn't do," said Kelly breathlessly.

The judge smiled gently, "You take care of them."

John turned to the boys: "Hey guys, I want you to know, that everything I said up there is true. I never thought I would get used to the idea of you, but now I couldn't imagine any other children I'd rather have."

"Um, about that. I have something I have to tell all of you," said Kelly anxiously. There was an uneasy smile on her otherwise glowing face.

"What?" asked Lane nervously. After all this, what could make her feel uneasy...

"I'm pregnant."

"What?!" exclaimed John. He grinned more with every word: "Wow...Oh my God! ...Three! ...Let's celebrate! Let's go out to eat ...Then we can start looking for a bigger house away from Dana ...We're going to have to start searching for baby equipment. And a tutor. And actual beds for the boys. And...college tuition..."

"John, we'll talk about all that later. Now, now let's just eat, I'm starving," laughed Kelly. She was holding her belly with one hand and Kid's hand tightly with the other, his eyes staring intently at her belly. "So, you're not mad?"

"Why would I be mad?"

"Well, this wasn't exactly the way I wanted to tell-"

"Wait," interrupted Lane. "So...so I'm gonna be a big brother?!"

"Something like that," smiled Will as he ruffled the boy's hair.

Although he wasn't completely sure what was to come, Will looked forward to the future. He was excited to see what it would bring. Someday maybe he would see his sister again. He would learn through his tutor and maybe even get into college; Lane at least would for sure. For now, he decided to put his past behind him and start a new life with Kelly and John. Hawk and Mad Dawg and the Jokers would always be his best friends, and he would always consider Ghost his ultimate protector and brother, but now he had a real family. It even said so on legal papers. He would soon be an older brother once again; for the third time with three separate couples. It would be weird when the baby was older, trying to explain how they had become it's brothers. But they would protect it and love it. It would be a good life.

20

One year later.

Will is now eighteen; Lane is ten. Their little sister, Diane, is just over four months. They moved into a house outside of the city, closer to the base where John works and farther from the trouble within the shadows of the skyscrapers. It has four bedrooms. Hawk and Mad Dawg visit a lot on weekends, and sometimes some of the other guys come down, too. Ghost is going to be out on parole in three weeks. Will, who should have been in his senior year of high school, is now in his junior year, on a five-year plan. He goes to a real high school with real students. Even though he feels overwhelmed a lot, he loves it there. It reminds him of before. Lane is being home-schooled now, but he will be starting in public school for sixth grade next year.

I am seventeen. I just recently applied to five colleges, for Social Work, but I'm not completely sure that I want to go. The reason being because my brother is not graduating yet. It was ironic, I was sitting in my Principles of Law class a couple of months ago, when in walks this guy. My friend Claudia leaned over and told me he was hot, with a goatee and easy muscles, and eyes that show deep into his soul, but I don't think he is at all. There's something about him that reminds me of a brother I once had. When he sees me, he makes a beeline towards me, making Claudia gasp. He sits next to me and we start talking. He's seventeen, too. He has just moved here with his guardians, but he's getting adopted in less than a month. He's an orphan as far as he can tell, but he has a little brother. Me too. He was homeless for a long time. I should have been. There is a strange expression on his face as he speaks to me. I think I have the same on my face even though I can't completely read it. I haven't yet said my name. Then he says:

"Your name is Hannah." I feel Claudia's eyes digging into the side of my skull, and my palms are sweating uncontrollably.

"Yeah."

"It wasn't a question. You know mine."

"Will," I manage before my voice breaks. He nods. Then we hug and I'm crying. Some of the kids look at us like we're lepers, but the girls are jealous of me and the guys are wondering what the hell just happened, if not what my boyfriend will say when he hears. When the teacher walks in she makes a crack about him moving fast, it being his first day and all. Then she realizes I'm crying. She asks what's wrong and I say absolutely nothing. Then I introduce her to my brother. Everyone becomes silent and watches what happens.

Everyone knows my story; I spent years trying to find them. A year earlier I had seen a story on the news. This creep had held a gun to this kid's head and they said a brief history of his life. I knew it was Lane. But I had not seen their faces, and they had not given names. And then when my adopted father tried to find them, he couldn't. They weren't legal parts of the city yet, I guess.

I imagined seeing him again so many times over the years, and then there he was. He just walks into my class. So now I think I might wait to go to college, but he doesn't want me to. He says I should go ahead as planned. We have a whole year to catch up. But there is so much I want to tell him and I don't think a year will be long enough to tell it all. I want to tell him how I went into foster care, but when my mom couldn't be found, my foster parents adopted me. But he had more to tell me. Claudia, my friend, wrote his story down. She's better at writing than me.

Lane asked to be called Kid Jax in it because "it's cooler" and to only use Lane if "you absolutely have to." I have to tell you, it was so crazy seeing him after all that time. He's so grown up now. He didn't even recognize me. Will told me later that he had barely remembered me, but he still talked about me all the time. He's cool. I wish I had seen him grow up.

Anyway, it's such a great story, and I didn't want to ruin it. It proves that nothing is too good to be true if you work for it to be so.

Nothing is too far out of reach.

It's just another star in the sky.

You just have to figure out some way to catch it.

Printed in the United States
56726LVS00006B/213

9 781424 145331